LET'S GET

naked

BEFORE WE SAY,

"I DO"

An Exploration of Needed Questions While Dating

DR. ANGELA HOOD, LMFT

ISBN: 978-0-578-30919-4

Contents

Preface.. v

Introduction : Get Naked? vii

Chapter 1   Why Bare All?.. 1

Chapter 2   Get Naked with Yourself! 9

Chapter 3   Discussing Awkward Questions 19

Chapter 4   What's in Your Future? 29

Chapter 5   What We Like to Do.....................................39

Chapter 6   Spirituality and Core Values 44

Chapter 7   Let's Talk about Money!...............................49

Chapter 8   Personality and Love Languages................59

Chapter 9   Our Health...74

Chapter 10   Relationships and Sexuality.......................84

Chapter 11   Are Children on the Menu?.......................95

Chapter 12   Roles, Divisions, and Decisions 105

Chapter 13   Families Shape Us 110

Chapter 14   Get Feedback! 115

Chapter 15   A Background Check?................................126

Conclusion.. 133

Preface

Are you new to the dating scene? Or have you experienced a series of dissatisfying relationships or gotten hurt? Have you just come through a painful divorce and are in a bit of a daze about starting over romantically? Perhaps you are fortunate enough to be in a happy long-term relationship and are thinking about marriage. Whatever your situation, you might be feeling like you can't trust yourself to make the right decisions.

I wrote this book because of the unhappy and even traumatic experiences that my clients and those dear to me have gone through. They thought they were in a great relationship with a wonderful person, but certain topics just never came up. Sadly, it didn't occur to them to ask the right questions.

Can you imagine discovering that your partner with whom you were in a relationship was born a different gender? Who would think to ask their partner, "What sex were you assigned at birth?" But in our fluid society, that needs to be added to the list! Another example would be asking about HIV/STIs, which can be an awkward conversation to have with anyone, let alone a potential lifelong partner. I mean, who wants to talk about STIs and HIV? However, it is better to know than not to know. Unfortunately, I have counseled multiple people who said, "I did not know, they never told me!" Because they had not engaged in candid dialog about sexual things, many of my clients were put at risk.

In another tragic case, a woman married a man who turned out to be a pedophile! She did not think to investigate his background before she welcomed him into her home to live with her and her children. Tragically, he raped her daughter. If only she had known more about him before she married him!

As a marriage and family therapist, I have heard sad stories about unhealthy relationships that could have been avoided had the right questions been explored. Unfortunately, they were too embarrassed or fearful of offending their love-interest to initiate those somewhat awkward discussions. They became hopelessly entangled with their partner – shared possessions, financial co-dependency, children – so they forged on with the relationship despite any misgivings.

Don't wait! If you delay too long in initiating the process, that relationship you're in may drift into a commitment you might regret later. Read through this book to discover the questions you need to be asking and how and when to ask them.

Introduction

GET NAKED?

hat's the secret to an enduring, passionate, healthy, and committed life-long relationship? The indispensable key to figuring out if that special person is *the one* is to "get naked" before you say, "I do." How do you get naked? By being real about who you really are – putting everything (well, nearly everything) out in the open and expecting your love interest to do the same.

To get naked means sharing past experiences, faults and frailties, opinions, spirituality, worldview, hopes and dreams and more. Admittedly, this is a bit counterintuitive when we first start hanging out with someone. We only want to put our best foot forward – we're terrified that if that other person really knew who we were, the relationship would go into slow fade.

Don't panic – you don't have to get completely naked on the first date – it's a process of conversations that take place over time – we'll discuss how it works in chapter three.

Getting naked empowers both of you and protects you from potential harm and heartbreak. It's a two-way street – you need to reveal the real you, and you also need to see your partner for who he or she really is. Often, in a new relationship, we tend to be so giddy with excitement that it's easy to overlook some important details about that person which need to be brought to light.

This book is about exploring topics that need to be explored – with candor and transparency. It's about having the courage to have those important conversations. This book supplies resources that will help you initiate and to shape dialogues that are informed, honest and open, and that ultimately will lead to happiness and wholeness in marriage.

Save yourself years of time wasted on a relationship that is unhealthy, unsatisfying, or years going nowhere. Five years from now you don't want to be saying, "If only I had known… (fill in the blank) …I would have never married him/her!" Avoid a lifetime of heartache and regrets by asking and answering questions to define your relationship. Know your partner well enough to decide if he or she is the person you want to wake up next to for the rest of your life.

WHY BARE ALL?

aring all will help you navigate through your relationship; it will prevent simply existing as a couple but never experiencing real true happiness. Through open communication over a wide variety of topics, you will be able to make wise and informed decisions about the future of your relationship, such as if this person is *the one*, or if you should run the other way as fast as you can.

One thing that may become clear is that you will need to be proactive in asking and answering important questions, and intentional and informed about commitments we make in a relationship.

Perhaps you're thinking, "Well, I don't want my partner to feel like I'm putting him (or her) through an inquisition. Isn't this sort of over-thinking things? Can't we just enjoy spending time together and let this relationship take us wherever it leads? Can't love make a way through any obstacles we might encounter?"

While it may sound beautiful and romantic to let the relationship unfold on its own, it's neither realistic nor healthy. And yes, it's fun to be a bit serendipitous when starting a new romance, as long as we don't get so caught up in the moment that we forget to consider how the consequences of decisions (or non-decisions) we make at this point will follow us for the rest of our lives.

If you wanted to climb Mount Everest, you wouldn't just hop on the first plane to Kathmandu, throw on a backpack, and start clambering up the slope. That would be fatal! You would first research all that's involved. How fit do you need to be? What sort of gear and equipment do you need, and are you experienced in handling them? When is the best time to climb? Do you have the mental strength to endure the hardship?

Before setting out on an adventure like this, you'd first need to know what questions to ask, and then figure out if the answers to those questions make you a good candidate for tackling the summit! The same could be said for approaching the adventure of a lifetime commitment to marriage – have you asked the right questions, and do you have the right answers?

Casually drifting

Today, the cultural norm for dating is a sort of casual slide from one stage to another – hanging out, starting sexual relations, occasionally spending the night, making the relationship "Facebook official," and eventually moving in together. It all just seems to happen, with little or no serious discussion. With minimal forethought, couples end up buying furniture and pets together, and some take on even greater commitments.

Planned or unplanned, forty percent of unmarried couples will have children together – almost as if, "Let's raise a couple kids, so we'll know if we're compatible enough for marriage." Should children really be the pawns in such uncertainty? About one-quarter of cohabiting couples will buy a home together. This state of "uncommitted commitment" may go on for years before it may (or most likely will not) end in marriage.

How is this working out? The good news is that the divorce rate is declining. But what is that really telling us? People must be married to get divorced, and that's only happening with twenty-six percent of individuals in their twenties and thirties.

What about the couples who are simply living together without marriage – are those relationships happy and lasting? Sadly, according to Pew Research, over half of the children of cohabiting couples will see their parents break up before they are nine years old, compared to only one in five of children of married couples.

Compared to married couples, studies show cohabiting couples have more dissension and conflict resolution issues and are more insecure about their partners' feelings, commitment, and future goals. Perhaps you're thinking, "Don't you have to live together first to confirm that you will be happily married?" No. Numerous studies show that couples who cohabit before marriage are about one-third *more* likely to get divorced than couples who did not live together prior to marriage.

Unhappy endings

A key reason many relationships don't work out is most couples slide from one stage of their relationship to another while bypassing the all-important discussions that should go along with these commitments, such as defining the relationship and learning salient details about their partner. Once they get entangled in the commitments involved in living together, especially if they have children or go into debt together, it becomes harder to get out of the relationship.

The "inertia effect" kicks in, and they end up sort of stuck together and may feel like they have no choice but to get married. After all, they've already invested so much time and have multiple commitments together. But then they may begin to wonder whether they had consciously chosen their partners, or if they had just allowed fate to take its course. Regrettably, many feel like they have made a mistake and married the wrong person.

Sexual relations-commitment

You might be considering it just a one-night stand. Or a little bit of fun with no strings attached. Or maybe the precursor to a potential long-term relationship. But sexual relations bring far more than erotic pleasure. The act of sex bonds the couple together, emotionally, and physically – through their hormones. This bond becomes stronger the more the couple has sex together.

The hormone *oxytocin* is released in the woman's brain, which relieves stress, creates feelings of closeness with her partner and the desire to nurture him. *Vasopressin* is a hormone primarily released in the brain of men during intimate relations. It's nicknamed the *commitment hormone* because it creates the desire to bond, be loyal and even jealous. Men and women also experience the release of *endorphins* – "happy hormones" – during sex, which can be addictive!

These hormones released through sexual intercourse help a married couple stick it out because of the bonding effect it creates between the couple – they get addicted to each other! However, these hormones can be problematic for two people who haven't any sort of commitment to the other and may not know each other well. Your hormones will cause you to develop a bond to that person, even if you find out very quickly that he or she isn't "the one."

This is one reason why some people stay in unhealthy relationships – when they are advised to escape the situation, you will hear them say, "But I love him!" That's the hormones (and perhaps an unhealthy dose of co-dependency) talking!

We will discuss sexuality in chapter ten, and specific topics that need to be candidly explored before engaging in sexual intimacy. It's critical to have those important conversations first, and to know your partner well enough that you can commit with confidence. If you jump into bed together right off the bat, your hormones will talk louder than your brain, and you may find yourself enmeshed in a relationship that you wouldn't have gotten involved in otherwise.

Swim against the tide

Baring all will help you swim against the tide of cultural norms. To safeguard against unhappy mistakes (and spending too much time on a mistake), be intentional about discussing your motivation and commitment level with your love interest – before you transition to that next stage of your relationship. You don't want to end up drifting into marriage with someone you're not completely sure about, so be proactive about knowing your partner well.

Perhaps you feel like it's a good idea, hypothetically, to have these discussions before commitment, but you are immobilized by fear. Fear of rejection if you reveal all, fear of being judged unworthy, fear of being alone. When we make decisions out of fear, or fail to act out of fear, we ultimately make ourselves victims in one way or another.

Having the courage to begin dialogues about sensitive issues will empower you as you take charge of your life and your future, rather than just drifting along with the tide. Celebrate opening those doors, letting in the light on areas you need to know about, and dispelling the darkness of uncertainty.

The first conversation you need to have is with yourself. *Know thyself!* We tend to attract others based on what we feel we deserve. If you feel unlovable or undeserving of the best, you may want to consider counseling for low self-esteem and other issues before jumping into romance. Develop a healthy self-identity. Know who you really are, and what you really want from life, and what you want in the person you will spend your life with.

Then, be proactive about discussing the topics covered in this book with your significant other as you move through your relationship. Have the courage to have those conversations about your core values, your goals, your preferred lifestyle, your finances, your spirituality, your individual personalities and love languages, your sexuality, past mistakes, and past relationships, having and raising children (including children you may already have), and your opinions about gender roles.

In addition, before things start getting serious, remember to ask questions of yourself about your partner. Are any red flags popping up? Finally, get feedback from your family and friends. Do they have any areas of concern about your love interest? Don't commit to advancing to the next stage of your relationship before you know what you need to know. The best time to work on your marriage is before you have one!

GET NAKED WITH YOURSELF!

Who are you?

efore getting involved in a romantic relationship, know who *you* are. Knowing yourself helps you figure out what you want in your life partner. Think about your passions, your goals, how well you get along with the people in your life, whether you have unhealed scars or unhealthy personality traits that need to be addressed, how past relationships have shaped you, and whether you're bringing anyone with you (such as children) into a relationship.

Dealing with any unresolved issues has intrinsic value in helping you develop a healthy romantic relationship. You don't want to find the perfect mate and then sabotage the relationship by a lack of clarity on who you are and how to relate well with others. When you know yourself well, you can identify your morals and values. When these are shared, they help shape healthy relationships, allow you to identify with others, and be secure and confident in a relationship.

Furthermore, knowing yourself will help you identify questions to explore with your partner before beginning a romantic relationship – and through its progression. Does that the person you're hanging out with share your core values, have complementary life goals and passions, and accept you for who you are? Understanding yourself helps you explore what characteristics in a potential mate are especially important to you, prevent you from compromising, and allows you to decide which characteristics would be deal-breakers.

What are your core values?

Your core values are your fundamental beliefs about life that guide your understanding of morality, dictate your behavior, decide your priorities and decision making, motivate your actions, and serve as a guide and measuring stick for what you want to achieve in life (and how well you're doing at it). Your core values define who you are and what brings meaning to your life, so you want to find someone who aligns with the values that are most important to you.

Your core values include your beliefs about God, how to steward your resources, how important family is to you, what you believe is good and evil, how much power you feel you have over your life, and what you think are the most important characteristics in a person. Your values are framed by your conscience, your faith, your family's lifestyle and beliefs, and input from others: teachers and other leaders through your life, your peers, books you've read, and the media.

The first thing you should consider when deciding your core values is what you believe about God, how important your faith is to you, and how important it is to you that your life partner shares your faith.

You should also ask yourself how your faith informs your morality and lifestyle, your sense of self and personal empowerment, your ideas about family life, and your goals for the future. If your faith (or lack of it) does not influence these matters very much, then you need to ask yourself what the driving force is behind your values. Chapter six will cover discussing your spiritual values with your significant other, but you need to be clear on where you stand first.

One thing you can do when considering your core values is review these personal attributes (and more will come to mind that you can add in) and ask yourself which are your "top five" – the most important attributes you hope others see in you. Then you can think about the "top five" that you want in your life partner (and the father or mother of your children). These will help you understand who you are, and frame in your mind the kind of person you want for a life partner.

Sample personal attributes: commitment, compassion, consistency, courage, creativity, education, efficiency, environmentalism, fitness, good humor, good looks, honesty, innovation, loyalty, motivation, open-mindedness, optimism, passion, perseverance, positivity, reliability, service to others, spirit of adventure.

What are your dreams?

What are you most passionate about? What are your aspirations in life? Do you have a series of goals that you have set to help you achieve your dreams and that you are actively working toward? What are you currently doing to fulfill the destiny that you believe is yours?

Perhaps you have some vague goals, but you are not doing much to make them happen. You first need to be precise on what you want to do with your life. Write your goals down from small to largest. Once you have written down your goals then write down what you need to do to carry out each specific goal. Began to tackle them one at a time by writing an accomplish date next to the goal you have completed before you move to the next goal. Trying to accomplish too many goals at once will only create unnecessary stress in your life.

Life goals fall into several categories. First, there's the

big dream – what you expect will be your ultimate contribution in life. Next, there are *short-term goals* – these are objectives that you intend to achieve fairly quickly – such as within the coming year, or by the end of three or four years – to move you forward toward the big dream. For example, if your dream job requires a college degree, one of your short-term goals will be to complete your degree.

Next, are the *90-day goals* – achievements that you intend to carry out within the next three months. Lastly, there are the *bite-sized goals* – what you intend to get done today or by the end of the week. These smaller and larger goals work together to help you realize your dreams in life.

Sometimes, as we travel through life, our dreams may change, or we might need to adjust some of our goals due to some sort of complication. But a life well lived is a life that is constantly moving forward. One conversation that you want to have with your potential life partner is about dreams and goals, and before you have that discussion, you need to be clear on what your own realistic dreams are, and what you're doing to make them happen.

Cracks in the foundation?

Cracks in a foundation destroy relationships, so before you get involved with another person, you need to be emotionally healthy, grounded, and authentic. You don't want to meet the ideal person and then push them away because you haven't fixed the cracks in your foundation, or you have deep-seated insecurities.

In preparation for looking for that special someone, take a good look at yourself and address any personal issues that might cause problems in the relationship. It's time to air things out, so you can find rest, freedom, and wholeness. What past experiences are still haunting you? What past relationship experiences are stopping you from experiencing true love? Are you struggling with your mental health? Do you have any addictive behaviors that you need to conquer? How is your relationship with your parents affecting you?

We all have struggles and matters that need to be settled, and there's no shame in that. But get help and get healthy before launching into a relationship. Pursue therapy if necessary. Otherwise, those cracks in the foundation will start to grow and eventually you and your partner will fall through.

Healthy non-romantic relationships?

Before you start looking for a life partner, think about the relationships you have now – such as with your parents, siblings, friends, classmates, colleagues, and roommates. These people shape you, affirm you, and help you discover the real you. Your relationships with them have hopefully taught you some important relationship skills such as communication, trust, and mature conflict resolution.

How well do you listen to these people and candidly share your own thoughts and opinions? Are you an encourager of people, or do you tend to be critical and negative? Do you give people your time, attention, and aid, or are you just a taker? Have you learned healthy ways of giving and receiving constructive feedback? Are you empathetic with them – are you able to perceive their feelings and needs? Do you treat them as you would like to be treated?

You may be thinking right now, "Well, my family is dysfunctional, so I don't spend much time with them, and a lot of people that I have gotten close to have hurt me, so I pretty much just keep to myself." If this is the case, you probably aren't ready to get involved in dating right now.

If you have not experienced and learned important skills from healthy non-romantic relationships, you will have impaired ability to successfully develop a romantic relationship. Consider working with a counselor on developing essential relationship skills, and also work on building up more social relationships so you can practice healthy skills.

Healthy relationship skills include attentive listening, appropriate communication, agreeably disagreeing, settling conflicts peacefully and kindly, being a giver and not just a taker, sharing and being a team player, and reading social cues. The more skillful you are in your non-romantic relationships, the better your chances of developing a happy and enduring relationship when you meet that special someone.

Past relationships

Have you suffered hurts and bruised ego in past relationships? Have you recovered from your last relationship, or are you still dreaming up ways to get that person back? If you are still licking your wounds or not over your ex, don't be unfair to someone else by jumping into a rebound relationship. Instead, use this time of healing to analyze what did and didn't work in past relationships. Consider what you may need to change in your own life to enjoy a successful romantic future.

When thinking about past relationships, ask how healthy they were. Were you constantly sacrificing what was important to you? Were you too needy? Did the two of you have trust issues? How did you handle conflict? If you weren't able to establish functional relationships in the past, take time to learn about healthy relationships. Look around at your relatives, friends, pastor, and others you know in "happy" marriages and observe and ask what makes them work.

Who's coming with you?

Do you have any children living with you from an earlier relationship or marriage? If so, you need to think about what sort of person would fit in well with your current family situation. At this point, you have to think beyond what is nice for you, to what is best for the whole family. Just because that other person is a lot of fun or the two of you have great chemistry does not mean that he or she is a good fit for your family.

You really don't want to have a whole parade of different people coming through your child's life that you haven't vetted well or who may not stay around long. Your priority should be supplying your children a safe and stable life.

You also need to take the thoughts and feelings of your child (or children) into consideration. Get their feedback about how they feel about you dating. If you and they have just experienced a painful divorce or breakup, they may be feeling lonely and insecure without their other parent in their daily lives. They may feel very possessive of you, and young children may feel angry or confused to see you with a new partner.

It's reasonable for them to want some time with just you. It's not a bad idea to take some time to recover from your past relationship before you move on to the next person. The more your value yourself the more other will also.

When you do start dating and have been going out with someone for a while, begin to include that person in activities with the children. Get feedback from your kids (depending on your children's age) on how they feel about that person. Pay attention to how well that person interacts with your kids, and how much interest they seem to have in parenting.

Who are you looking for?

A lot of your criteria for your future life mate are a matter of individual preference. However, having a good perception about who you are at your core, and what you need and what you desire in life will aid you in defining what kind of person you want to spend your life with.

Obviously, you want someone who embraces the core values that are most dear to you. As we go through this book and discuss different topics, you will achieve even greater clarity about the kind of person you want to marry. As we cover the variety of topics to discuss with your significant other before marriage, you will start to think about things that never occurred to you and begin to form a picture in your mind of the kind of person you really want to marry.

DISCUSSING
AWKWARD
QUESTIONS

ne reason that couples don't engage in these important discussions is that they just don't know
how to do it! You may be confused about when
it's appropriate to talk about various subjects. You may feel
embarrassed about bringing certain sensitive topics up or
how to get a conversation started on some issues.

Maybe you've tried to broach some subject, and just
gotten a non-response from your partner. And then there's
that ever-so-scary thought that the answer might not be
what you want to hear! This chapter will help you sort
out when to talk about what, how to ask those awkward
questions, and what to do if your partner isn't opening

up or you get an answer that might be a relationship deal-breaker.

Timing is everything!

Deciding when to ask the right question while dating during a budding relationship is important but when and how to ask those question is just as important. Some questions are appropriate (and ought to be addressed) either before or on your first date, some are suitable for the first few weeks of dating, and some quite pertinent as you start getting serious and start making key life decisions.

Earlier I talked about topics you want to discuss with your partner as you're getting to know each other and versus topics you should discuss as your relationship deepens. However, with each topic, there's questions that should be addressed fairly soon, and others that can wait.

Before you embark into a new relationship it is important that you have an idea of what your goals are for the future, what you are passionate about doing with your life, and what you've been doing to make these goals a reality – such as with your education and job experience.

It's natural on a first date (or even before, as you're chatting online or on the phone) to discuss your jobs and career aspirations, if you're in college or have completed a degree, and so forth. It is *not* natural but necessary to ask about STI's. We don't ask the difficult questions because we don't want to run the individual away before moving on to the next phase of the relationship.

You don't need to divulge details of every dating relationship you've had, but you don't want to waste your time or the time of the person you're interested in either. This is why it is important to know your value and worth. The worst thing you can do is wait until you have feelings for someone to start playing the game "have you ever."

I remember watching a television show called *90 Day Fiancé*, and a guy proposed to the young lady. However, she did not disclose she was still married to her ex-husband. Here is a tip: if you've been married or if you have any children, those are topics that need to be covered right off.

Another tip about timing is to jump on opportunities to explore a topic further when it comes up naturally in conversation or in a particular situation you're going through. For instance, your new partner mentions that they just got off the phone with their sister. This will create an opportunity to ask questions about their family. For example, you can say something like, "That's cool -- are you close to your sister?" "How often do you speak with her?" "Which one of you is the bossy one?" "How would you describe your relationship with her?" and so forth.

Asking those type of questions will help you learn something about their family life and relationship skills. They may even start up a whole discussion about their family dynamics as a springboard off one or two questions from you. Also, you could say, "I'd love to meet your sister!

Why don't we all go out for brunch or something." You want to get to know your partner's family, because the apple does not fall far from the tree.

A third tip is maximizing the right time for productive discussions. If he or she just got home from work and is stressed out, that's not a good time. If they are in the middle of watching their favorite show or game that is not a good time. Choose times when the two of you are both relaxed and have a block of time where you can talk, such as when you're having a meal or going on a walk together.

I like to encourage my clients to schedule a table talk. Take one day out of the week where you both are less likely to be busy and let that day be the day you discuss all of your major thoughts and concerns for the week (this does not apply to emergency situations). Using the appropriate time to have a discussion is more effective than spur of the moment.

Ask open-ended questions

It takes considerable skill to phrase questions that aren't threatening and to know how to ask questions that encourage explanation and discussion. But this is a skill that will serve you well in life, not only in your marriage, but with your career, friends, and other relationships.

Open ended questions create room for a deep and meaningful conversation as well as allow your partner to think from a higher abstract level. Here is a tip to remember: open-ended questions start with *W* and *H* – What, When, Where, Why, Who, Which and How.

When asking open-ended questions, the use of *how* will elicit a feeling, frequency, or emotional response; whereas *what* will allow an individual to respond using actualities. *When* and *where* are questions that are looking for a specific place, period of time, and sequences.

Avoid questions with "yes" or "no" answers. Instead, begin your questions with phrases like, "what do you think…" or "tell me about…" For example, if you want to know more about your girlfriend's past, you could ask "What is one of your favorite memories from your childhood?" And, then you can ask more open-ended questions when she answers. If she says, "Well, I always loved it when we went camping in the mountains," then you could ask, "What was the best part of those camping trips for you?"

What if they don't open up?

Some people are very private individuals and just aren't used to talking about themselves. Other people are just quiet – they don't talk about much at all, or they just don't trust you enough to share intimate things about themselves. Still others aren't used to voicing their opinions about things. They may have grown up with families where communication is not encouraged. And then, you might meet someone who's hiding something about themselves or about their past. So, part of the issue here is discerning why they aren't opening up.

If you find that they are a voracious talker about some things – for instance, they'll go on and on about sports, fashion, or music, and have very decided opinions about these things, but they clam up when you ask them something more personal about themselves, then you can probably narrow it down to they're either very private *or* they're hiding something. So, what to do? How do you know which is the issue?

One way is to spend time with their family or friends. You can learn a lot about the person from their parents, siblings, and children (if they have any) – both about their personality and whether they're hiding something.

A lot of times, the family members might just blurt something out, and you can also encourage them, such as, "Tell me a funny story about *(name)* when he/she was a kid" or "What kind of kid was *(name)*? Was he/she always getting into trouble or was he/she the model child?" If you continue to have concerns, you might consider running a background check, especially if it's someone you haven't known long.

Another way you can find out is play a game like the "Ungame" (there's even a couple's version) or "Never Have I Ever." This is a great way to get your partner to talk in a non-threating way. You can also ask them, "Tell me something about you that you have never told any other date."

Even if the person isn't hiding something and is just

very private or reluctant to open up about his or her feelings or opinions – consider if this something you can tolerate in a serious relationship. It's unlikely that they're going to change their personality, and you really don't want to be banging your head on the wall in frustration when they are unwilling or unable to open up.

A troublesome response?

This is one reason why you need a good understanding of your own core values, so you can decide if their response is a deal-breaker for you. Let's face it – no couple agrees on *everything* –some diversity of opinion or habits keeps things interesting. But some things are just so much a part of who you are that you need someone who shares that with you. For instance, if your faith is especially important to you, you need someone who's on the same page.

Another example of a deal-breaker might be a career choice that you can't live with. Let's say, for instance, that your partner is career military, and likely to be moved to one base after another – around the world or around the country, and your own career requires you to live in certain major cities where your company is located. You're going to have to decide if one of you can change your career and be happy with that.

This is one reason why it's important to have these conversations – early on. You don't want to fall hopelessly in love with the person, and then discover there's something about them you can't live with.

Observe and listen!

You can learn a lot about your new love interest's values by observing and listening. I have had to learn the hard way by listening more and talking less. The first question is to ask yourself is, "What am I listening for?" Are you listening to learn more about your partner? Are you listening to find fault because the relationship is too good to be true or are you listening to prepare your rebuttal?

Most people select what they want to hear instead of what their partner is saying. Intentional listening can lead to a healthy conversation and relationship. So, what should you be listening for? You want to listen for information. Take finances, for example. You want to learn how your partner handles their finances. You can ask, what are your views relating to a person who lives for the moment versus putting aside for a rainy day?

You are listening for information on if they run through their paycheck quickly, or if they talk about putting some funds aside? Do their spending habits match up with their income? If they have a modest income but are frequently going to high-end restaurants, wearing designer clothing, or driving expensive cars, that's an indicator that they're likely deeply in debt. Listen to how they talk about their respect towards money.

Ask non-threatening questions.

One way to phrase non-threatening questions is to use non-questions. For example, state a fact about yourself or about an opinion you have about something, and then just pause…and wait to see if they respond with a similar fact about themselves or their own opinion on the topic.

For instance, you might say something like, "Well, today I sat down and made up a plan for getting my school loans paid off. I'm giving bigger payments to the smaller balances, and just paying the minimum payment on the others." A statement like this will probably generate a response something like:

a. Oh yeah? Well, my school loans are a lost cause! I'm in serious default!
b. That sounds like a great plan! Maybe you could show me how to do that with my loans.
c. Yes! That's what I've been doing too! I've already got two large loans paid off, and only a few thousand to pay off.

Each of these responses gives you helpful information about your partner's approach to debt-reduction. The first answer reveals a person that is unmotivated (or unable) to get out of debt and probably has a low credit score. The second answer reveals a person who is open to improving their skills in debt reduction and working together with you in learning more. The third person probably already has sound financial planning skills.

Another way to ask non-threatening questions is to inquire about their opinion on something. For instance, if you want to know more about their core values, and someone posts something on Facebook or says something on the news, you could ask your partner how they feel about that statement, which could generate a discussion about values. You could phrase that question something like this: "I heard/read something interesting today and I wanted to know your thoughts on that."

WHAT'S IN YOUR
FUTURE?

ou don't need to have the same career goals or passions as your future spouse, but these things do need to be complementary. By this, I mean that your goals and passions need to be in harmony with the person you want to spend your life with.

When two people are in a complementary relationship they complete each other – they mutually supply whatever is lacking in the other, so that each person is better for being in the relationship, and the couple are able to work together to achieve their calling in life. In this chapter, I will suggest questions to explore with your new love interest, preferably at the beginning of the relationship (with the exception of the last section on setting goals together).

Life calling

This doesn't necessarily mean career goals, although those might be included. Your calling in life means where your lives are headed, what each of you are passionate about, and how your individual callings line up with each other. Exploring your calling in life means to think about who you are and why you are on this earth and what you want to achieve with your life.

The two of you can have mutual passions but different career goals and different ways of achieving your calling. Let's say you both are passionate about helping people with disabilities. One of you might be a speech therapist helping disabled people communicate better. The other might assist fundraising events supporting the disabled or volunteer in an adaptive sports program for special needs kids. You would have different jobs, but shared passions.

When you have a shared passion, you're able to support and encourage each other, and be better at achieving your calling in life together than if you were on your own. You have a natural connection – things you are both highly interested in talking about – and free-time activities that you enjoy doing together.

This is one reason why you want to talk about this early in the relationship, because mutual passions lead to healthier relationships. You might have met a fantastic person, but they may not be fantastic for you if they have no interest whatsoever in what makes you tick.

That being said, they might possibly acquire an interest in your life passion – to the point that it becomes their calling as well. It might be something that they'd not given much thought to prior, but through knowing you they may become as enthusiastic about it as you are. But you'd want to be sure they're not just trying to placate you. You need to get this sorted out before you get too invested in the relationship.

Career goals

You've probably had a job interview where you were asked, "Where do you think you'll be five years from now?" And this is a great question to ask each other – where do you expect to be five years from now, and doing what? What about ten years from now?

This could even be a first-date question. It's natural to talk about your current jobs on your first date or even prior to your first date. But for many young people, their current job isn't necessarily their life ambition. They may just be working to get themselves through college or may be working at a job to get experience that will be a stepping-stone to their future career goal.

There are several reasons why you want to discuss current and future (and even past) jobs. First, you want to know that the person is financially independent – able to live on their own earnings. Secondly, your career could have an impact on where you live (some jobs require a specific location), your standard of living, and how much traveling is involved. Your career usually has an impact on how available you are to care for your children.

A person's job history can give a sign of their stability. Have they worked the same job for some time, or are they constantly job hopping? And if so, why are they always changing jobs? This could give some insight into issues like poor conflict resolution skills, poor work ethic, problems with focus and prioritizing, or perhaps an inner restlessness and need for constant change.

So, you do want to explore information about their current job and what their plans are for their career. What are they doing right now to make that goal a reality? If they aren't doing anything, that's something to think about.

For instance, they may say that their life goal is to be a veterinarian, but they're working as a barista in a coffee shop and have no experience with even volunteering at an animal shelter. They aren't doing anything to achieve this goal, so you can deduce that it's not something they're seriously pursuing. And that might make you question whether they have a good understanding of themselves and if they know how to take steps to achieve their goals.

Educational goals

They may have finished high school, been trained in a job skill, and are done with school. They may have completed a college degree but are planning to pursue post-graduate studies. The important thing is that they've either achieved their educational goals or are working diligently to do so.

If you're ready to settle down soon, and they still have another four years of school or more, that's something to give thought to. It's best to have most of the education process behind you before you marry, because it's hard to manage going to school when caring for children and having to work enough to pay the bills at the same time. It's possible, and some people manage, but it does create a lot of stress for family life.

Another thing to consider about career and educational goals is the standard of living you want to have. Some people are perfectly content with living a modest lifestyle, while others want to have an elegant home, lovely wardrobe, and other material things. So, first, you need to find out whether the other person shares your views about lifestyle, and whether one or both of you has the education and career to support it.

Bucket list

Beyond your life's calling and your educational and career goals, there might be other things you really want to achieve in life. Sometimes we call this a "bucket list" – things you want to do before you die – such as travel to Alaska, run a half- marathon, or learn how to jump on a pogo stick. Many of these are a bit whimsical, but others represent a deep interest the person has, which impacts their life and free time.

For instance, an avid birdwatcher might want to complete a "life list" of bird species that they've been able to spot around the country. This means that future vacations might involve sitting for hours on the side of the road next to a forest while your significant other is staring at the trees through binoculars, trying to spot an elusive warbler. It's important to learn each other's life goals, especially ones that will consume a lot of time and expense.

Past mistakes

There are many mistakes in the past that might cause a problem with achieving one's goals in life, including a criminal past, debt, and poor credit score, lots of job hopping, or flunking out of school.

For example, one young woman completed her medical degree and began practice as a psychiatrist. Soon, she became romantically involved with one of her patients and in an unethical financial situation. She had to relinquish her medical license for seven years, and then she had a "black mark" on her record. The only work she could get was as a psychiatrist in a men's prison, until eventually, years later, she started a private practice in a remote town. Her mistakes of the past had a significant effect on both her career and her marriage.

This is just one example of how an error in judgment

can haunt a person and their career and their family life for years, so it's best to get these things out in the open before getting too involved in a relationship.

What does tomorrow look like?

Having a strong and healthy relationship is a beautiful thing. This kind of relationship will weather storms and emerge victoriously. However, this kind of relationship is not built overnight. It demands dedication and hard work from both of you.

Perhaps you've been dating for a number of months or even more than a year. You've already discussed your passions, your career goals and other life goals and what you're doing to achieve them. Your relationship is developing well. You're moving beyond the heady rush of excitement you had in the early weeks of your relationship, and you have more clarity about who each other is – you see their faults but also their strengths.

Now it's time to take the discussion about goals for the future to the next step – moving from the individual goals each of you have for yourself to where you see your future as a couple going.

What are your goals as a couple? What milestones do you hope to achieve together? Happiness emerges when you have something to look forward to – when you are moving toward that which you desire. Many couples make the mistake of making the wedding the "end goal." They are more excited about their wedding plans than where their marriage will be one year later.

You need to extend your focus to one year, five years, and ten years or more beyond the wedding. You've already asked each other about where they see their career going five or ten years from now – now it's time to ask yourselves that of your relationship – "Where do you see your marriage five years from now?" By setting realistic goals with one another you are setting your relationship up for victory.

Couple goals

Here are practical steps you can take to begin the discussion and build a relationship that is firm, robust, and stable.

Step 1: By now, you should have already discussed your individual personal goals. It is important that your individual goals align with your goals as a couple, so you can create a loving atmosphere that allows both of you to reach your dreams.

Step 2: Discuss how and where you want to be in the next six months to two years. Let your imagination run wild for a bit before you begin gleaning the real goals from this picture. Now extend your imagination to the next three years after that and do the same again. Be sure to keep your ideas both positive and practical

Step 3: Check to ensure that both of you feel passionate and positive about the goals you are setting as a couple. It is never good to try fulfilling goals that are not in sync with your personal goals. Your personal goals and your couple goals should be complementary – benefiting each other so that your relationship becomes a powerful catalyst for realizing your calling in life.

Step 4: Review your goals to confirm that they are attainable, specific, and realistic. Anything else gives room for bitterness when you fail to achieve your goals. It's wiser to set goals that are grounded and even a bit modest. You will experience the thrill of victory as you achieve these goals and perhaps even exceed your expectations.

Step 5: Each time the two of you accomplish any goal, no matter how small, celebrate it! Agree on a reward system to ensure that both of you stay motivated on developing your relationship and future together.

Step 6: Create a system that leaves each of you accountable to your commitments – both individual and as a couple. When we go through difficult times in our lives, it's easy to abandon some of our dreams, so this system of mutual accountability will help you stay the course and achieve your objectives.

Step 7: Come to an agreement about how to share and accept feedback, in order to improve as a person as well as to improve the relationship.

Step 9: Write down and review your goals from time to time. By writing and going back to them, you are becoming accountable for them. Research shows that people who write down their goals achieve more of them than those who did not.

Step 10: Your goals should include taking on projects with your partner. Doing things together is a great way to get more things done while enjoying each other's company and learning from (and about) each other. When you're finished, you have a sense of triumph in something you achieved as a unit.

By setting goals in your relationship, you are giving it every reason to grow and blossom. It will help nurture your relationship beyond the honeymoon phase to flourish and grow for many years to come.

WHAT WE LIKE TO DO

This chapter is about exploring each other's preferred lifestyle. A high percentage of people list "walks on the beach" as a favorite activity on their dating profile, but how often do you actually do that, especially if there isn't a beach within a hundred miles? What do you really do with your free time and what does your typical day look like? These sorts of questions are a better measure of how well-matched you are.

You don't necessarily have to like all of the same things, and you may come to enjoy new activities as a result of the relationship, but you need to have enough commonalities in your preferred lifestyle that you actually enjoy being with each other. These are all questions you can have fun exploring at the very beginning of the relationship. Most differences won't be deal-breakers, but some may – it's up to you to decide what you can and cannot live with.

Everyday lifestyle

Are you an early riser or sleep to noon? Are you okay with a messy house or do you a place for everything and everything in its place? Are you a homebody or do you love to get out and do something every day after work? Couch potato or exercise buff? Watch TV or read books? Classical music or heavy metal? Spicy food?

These are all personal lifestyle preferences that are probably somewhat important to you. It's unlikely that you'll be perfectly matched in all areas, so it's important that both of you have some flexibility so you can adapt to each other's preferences, and also important that you know which of these can be problematic if you're on different ends of the spectrum.

For instance, if one of you loves to get up at 4:30 every morning to have several hours to exercise, pray, pay bills, and read the news before leaving for work, will you be able to do that without judging (or disturbing) the other who rolls out of bed at the absolute last minute? And what about when you get home in the evenings and one of you wants to just put on their jammies and collapse on the couch, and the other wants to go out and have some fun?

Food is an interesting part of the relationship – it can be something that brings you together, or it can kind of drive you apart. What if you love exploring all sorts of ethnic foods and spices, and the other just wants plain food or is a super-picky eater? Or your partner is totally into paleo, gluten-free whole foods, and your secret pleasures are tater tots and frozen pizza? Let's face it – if you are married, you're going to be eating together most days, so best to get that sorted out.

I have been married for twenty-one years, and my husband and I have argued many times over food because he likes plain food, and I am a foody who wants to explore different types of cuisine. My son is just as picky as my husband, so I cook three different meals for us all to eat.

Weekends and vacations

What do each of you typically do on a Saturday? Do you spend the day cleaning house, doing laundry, and shopping, and mowing the lawn? Or are you off on an adventure somewhere – to the beach or a hike or kayaking down the river? Or maybe hosting a big party? And what about Sundays? Is church an important part of your regular weekly habits, or do you prefer to sleep in and then get brunch?

How much alone time do each of you need? Do you want to be joined at the hip with your partner all the time? And how do each of you feel about spending time with other people – for instance, the guy might want to hang out with his buddies watching sports or going off on a fishing trip, and the lady might want to have time with her girlfriends shopping or going to the spa or the movies. Are both of you comfortable with spending time apart from each other doing things with other people?

What do each of you prefer to do for vacations? Do you like to save up and splurge on a special trip or cruise, or do you usually visit family, or do you stay home and catch up on projects? If you do go on a special trip, is it going to involve a lot of rest and relaxation – like sitting at the pool or beach, or do you want high action – like zip-lining or rock climbing or hitting the streets?

What about pets?

Do you have any pets? How do you feel about owning a pet? Do you have asthma or allergies that would make pet ownership a problem? If you both like having a dog or a cat, what about rules for where those animals can and cannot go? Will you allow the dog on the sofa or the cat on the kitchen counter or either on the bed with you? Who's going to feed the animal, take it to the vet, groom it, clean the poop, and buy food for it?

I remember during the early stages of my marriage we lost three dogs because I was unwilling to have anything to do with dogs. It wasn't that I didn't like the dogs. It was because I never felt safe around them, therefore, I did not know how to treat them. This caused a problem in my relationship with my husband.

It's fairly important to explore all the nuances of your personal preferences fairly early on – and it will help you learn more about the other person. One thing that is super important for both of you is being flexible and adaptable.

For one thing, you're never going to find someone who is the perfect match in every single area of your preferred lifestyle – so you're going to have to compromise on some things – and that's actually a good thing, because life tends to throw a lot of surprises and changes our way (especially when babies show up), and we all must make accommodations for those changes, so adaptability is a good attribute to develop.

But some words of caution – are you doing all the accommodating? Or are you expecting your partner to bend to your every whim? Both are red flags – you should both be practicing flexibility and adaptability. If one of you is doing all the accommodating, that might mean that one of you has an underdeveloped sense of self-worth and/or it might mean that one partner is overly dominating.

Another caution is to think about differences you can live with and what issues would be deal-breakers for you. Would it drive you insane if your mate is constantly leaving a big mess everywhere? Or if you are a super-social person and your loved one just wants to spend quiet evenings at home? Only you can answer those questions, but be sure you do – before you say, "I do!"

SPIRITUALITY AND CORE VALUES

When a survey of marriage and family counselors asked which factors were the most important for a resilient marriage, they unanimously brought up faith and moral values. Maybe you don't think about these things very much now, but they play a bigger role in the strength of the marriage than you might expect.

Conflict often occurs in marriages when one person turns out to be much more committed to their faith than the other. This especially becomes an issue as children arrive, and you are making decisions about how to raise them. Remember to talk about your faith and your core values from the very start of your relationship, and as things progress, talk about how you see them affecting your shared life.

In Chapter 2 (Get Naked with Yourself), you were advised to explore your own core values, so that you have a concrete understanding of what you believe about God and how your faith informs your life decisions and morality. Now it's time to explore how the other person feels about these things, and how closely you are matched in your values and spirituality – the beliefs that guide your behavior, priorities, and goals, which motivate you to action, and bring meaning to your life. Here are questions to ask.

How important is your faith to you?

Share with each other what you believe about God, and how much that belief (or lack of it) impacts your core values. As you're doing this, you should share specifics about your preferred form of your faith – for instance, if you are a Christian, what type of Christian are you? Are you Catholic? Charismatic? Conservative? This is important because different denominations have different belief systems.

Must your life partner share your faith?

The two of you need to discuss how important it is that both of you share the same belief system. And maybe you'll say, "Well, you do your thing and I'll do mine" – but what about when the children come along? Will you take them to church, temple, mosque, or whatever your faith center is, and how often? If the two of you have different faiths (like if one of you is a Christian and the other is Muslim), how will you raise the children?

And don't say you'll just let the children decide, because they would have to be exposed to both belief systems to make an informed decision, and that could get really complicated. And even now, which holidays will you observe? If you both do share the same religion, but one of you has a vibrant faith, and the other is just a nominal believer, how do you feel about that? How is that going to work out long-term?

What are your spiritual habits?

If you do have a faith, how often do you go to your church or faith center? Every week? Or just once every month or so? Or just Christmas and Easter? Do you want your partner to come with you, or are you okay with just attending on your own?

Maybe both of you love going to church, but do you have different ideas about theology or your preferred worship style. Maybe one of you prefers conventional hymns and a pipe organ, and the other likes contemporary worship with drums and guitar. How will you work this out?

Are you involved with any ministries in your church or faith center – such as teaching Sunday school or singing in the choir? If your partner isn't involved in church, will they be jealous of the time you're spending there? And what about your daily habits? Are reading scripture, praying and/or meditating part of your regular routine? How does the other person feel about that? Is that something you would feel comfortable doing together?

Are core values in sync?

What drives your moral code – how do you decide what is good and what is evil? Your faith? Cultural and society norms? Something else? If one of you is diligently following the teachings of their faith with regard to morality, and the other has no faith, or maybe just a basic belief about God that doesn't really affect their lifestyle, will that be an issue?

Think about how any differences in your moral code will affect you right now as well as down the road when you are rearing your children. Let's take honesty for example – do you believe the occasional white lie is okay? What do you believe are the most important traits for a person to have? (Remember the list of attributes from Chapter 2, such as compassion, efficiency, service to others, innovation, etc.). What will you teach the kids?

And while we're talking about children, let's talk about marriage and family – how will your faith and your core values impact your family life? Do you believe in waiting until marriage before becoming sexually active, and are you in agreement on this? And how important is having children? Does one of you envision a houseful of kids, and the other thinks children are too intrusive and only wants one child or none? How committed are each of you to absolute sexual fidelity to one's spouse? How about your responsibility to your parents, especially in their old age?

Before you walk down the aisle together (and ideally, before you go out on another date together), it's really essential that the two of you identify your core values and whether you are in agreement. We've already talked about faith and morality. What about other core values?

Does one of you have a strong desire to accumulate wealth, while the other is happy to live a simple and carefree life with more focus on time with the family? What about generosity? Does one of you love giving lavish gifts, regularly contributing to charity and your church, and freely lending money, while the other tends to be a bit closed-fisted? How about kindness? Do you feel like your partner is kind to a fault – and that others take advantage of them? Which is more important to you – having power over others or pursuing peace? Does one of you need to be constantly busy, while the other values tranquility and simply sitting still?

Your faith and core values have an incredible impact on whether your relationship will be compatible, joyous, and enduring. Take the time before you get emotionally involved to have candid and transparent dialogue about your faith and values, so you can gain insight into whether this is a relationship that's wise to pursue.

LET'S TALK ABOUT MONEY!

Among the top three issues that married or co-habiting couples fight about is money. Finances are a common source of stress and tension, even in the most loving relationships. If you want to avoid arguments or financial disaster down the road, you need to start talking about some aspects of finances fairly soon into the relationship, and definitely get everything out on the table before getting into financial commitments together or getting married.

If you don't talk about money, there's a good chance that some really troubling issues might not come to light until you're co-mingling your finances. Your own credit score might be ruined, or you may suffer grave financial loss by decisions you make with your partner without knowing their financial habits.

One young woman had been dating a man for a few months, and she was madly in love. He convinced her to move with him away from her family to a different part of the country, where they were to invest in a new business. She went along with the plan; however, after she handed over her entire savings for this "investment," he suddenly disappeared in the middle of the night – and she never saw him or her money again. To make matters worse, she discovered she was pregnant with his child. She had to depend on the kindness of strangers to help her and her son when he was born.

By opening up about your financial situation with your partner, you are building a relationship on the solid foundation of honesty and communication. If one of you is hiding aspects of your finances from the other, it can lead to significant strains in your relationship down the road. By this, I don't just mean any debts you might have or a poor credit score, but also things like your habits of spending and saving. It's best to eliminate any unwanted surprises by being open and honest about these somewhat sensitive matters.

When to talk about finances?

You might feel it's a bit crass to ask questions about financial issues on the first date, or even in the first few weeks of a relationship. However, as we noted in chapter 3, this is a time when you can begin accumulating information by observation and listening.

Since you probably are talking about your jobs right off the bat, you may have a ballpark idea of the other person's income. You're also most likely discussing any college experience you've had, so this may give you some idea of any school loans that your new love interest may have. He or she may have had their education paid for by their parents, had some great scholarships, or worked their way through school – but those details may come out in early conversations in a natural way.

By carefully listening to their comments and observing their spending habits, and if they tend to be lending or borrowing money a lot, you can glean more information about where they are financially.

After you have been dating exclusively for some weeks, if everything is going well with the relationship, and it looks like things might become serious, then it's time to start having some frank discussions. You don't necessarily need to grill your special someone, but bring things up in a casual way, such as by talking about how you put together your own budget or your savings plan, and then pause…and allow your partner to comment about their own situation.

Don't delay too long to have these sorts of conversations. You don't want to be deeply in love and seriously involved, and then discover your loved one is hundreds of thousands in debt because of reckless spending or ill-advised investments and has a terrible credit score. By time you have been dating someone for several months, you should have a good grasp of:

- whether they are spending more than they're earning,
- if they more of a spender or more of a saver,
- whether they have a habit of making rash and expensive purchases,
- if they are paying their bills on time,
- if they're paying off the balance on their credit cards each month,
- if they have a high amount of debt and what they're doing about it,
- if they own any property,
- if they have a working budget, and are sticking with it fairly well, and
- if they have realistic financial goals (i.e., living debt free, buying a home, building wealth, etc.) and are taking steps to achieve them.

Sometimes, when we come from different socioeconomic backgrounds, we may have grown up with differing financial behaviors, so this needs to be taken into context when discussing financial things. We also need to remember that many young people are a bit irresponsible with their finances, but as they mature and begin to understand the importance of paying off debt, saving money and building a good credit score, they take steps to be more responsible. Having a not-so-great credit report isn't the end of the world; the important thing is that they are willing to change their ways and are actively taking steps to improve their financial standing. Exploring financial issues with your partner is inevitably awkward and difficult, but sometimes we just have to plow through as gracefully as possible.

Each of you needs to divulge your entire financial situation before co-mingling your finances in any way (like signing a lease together or taking out a car loan together), and before getting engaged and/or moving in together. In fact, you should realize that if you are co-mingling your finances, or going into debt, or making expensive purchases together (such as for appliances or furniture) without the legal protection of marriage, you might end up with complications.

Should you split up, you don't have the legally prescribed methods of dividing property that you would if you were married. If, God forbid, your lover becomes mentally incompetent (such as from a head injury), your lover's family – not you – would have the right to make decisions for him or her, including financial decisions. If your partner should die, you would have no claim to anything that you weren't a legal co-owner of – it would all go to your lover's family, not you, unless a will was written specifying you as the heir.

Be very careful about getting financially entangled with your significant other without carefully reviewing their financial record, and if their record is poor, be very careful about getting entangled at all. If, for instance, they have a bad credit score, it will affect the interest rate on any loans or mortgages you take out together.

One young woman encountered this when she and her lover decided to move in together. Because she had a clean credit history, and he had a lot of issues with his, she signed the lease and got utilities hooked up under her name. But when the relationship went sour, and he suddenly moved out, she couldn't afford to pay the lease and utilities without his income. She had to give up the apartment and sleep on a friend's couch for months. But now her own credit score was messed up, and she owed a debt to the utility company, which kept increasing because of fines until it became unmanageable and kept her from renting another apartment.

At the point where you are talking about serious commitment, you need to set aside your emotional attachment, and be as level-headed as possible – supporting the relationship yet protective of your interests. Items which you should review before marriage or making any sort of financial commitment together would include:

- credit history and credit score
- credit card debt

- any child support (including any unpaid back support)
- salary and other income
- any property he or she owns, and any mortgages (including 2nd mortgage) and liens
- any unpaid taxes (income tax, property tax, etc.)
- any unpaid bills, such as utilities, along with fines for non-payment
- any educational loans, car payments or other debt
- any bankruptcy
- any money owed to family members or friends

By laying all your cards on the table, you now know what is what. After reviewing these items, you may find aspects of your partner's economic history or conduct that is disturbing. You need to get out of your emotional cloud and take practical measures to turn the tables around and fix the financial problems. If your partner is unable or unwilling to fix things, then you need to seriously consider leaving the relationship before you experience financial ruin yourself.

What else?

Beyond understanding your partner's financial background and habits, you should also have a good understanding of his or her values and opinions with regard to money. Ask these questions of each other:

- Is saving money and/or investing money important to you?

- Are you willing for one or both of us to work extra hours now to get financially stable or save up enough for a down payment, even if it means less time together?

- How do you feel about loaning money to others? How much would you be willing to lend? Would you ever borrow money from family or friends? If so, how much?

- (If getting married) Do you prefer to pool all of our money from both incomes into one bank account from which all bills are paid, or have separate accounts and split the bills? Or use one income for weekly/monthly bills and expenses and the other for more occasional expenses, like taxes, home repairs or more expensive purchases and vacation?

- How will we decide how to spend money? Will we have some sort of agreement like any purchases over $50 or $100 will need to be agreed on by the other person?

Each couple must decide for themselves what their money strategy should be – there's no right or wrong answers. It all depends on your values and specific situation. But the important thing is that you need to clearly and reasonably communicate about financial things, live within your means, and do what works for you.

Red flags for financial abuse?

Some individuals feel that it's okay to leave the financial aspects of the relationship to the other person. Such decisions can lead to issues of control or deceit. You don't have to make your finances the center of your relationship, but you need to both be involved in financial decisions and clear about what is happening with the money. If any of the following situations are happening in your relationship, you are probably the victim of financial abuse.

- Your partner is controlling all the money.
- You have no say in how money is spent or how bills and debts are being paid.
- You don't know how much money is in the bank account or how much debt is owed.
- Your partner is only giving you what you need for specific items and not allowing you to have money to spend as you wish.
- Your partner discourages you from taking a full-time or high-paying job (making you financially dependent on your partner).
- Your partner does not allow you to have your own credit card.
- Your partner is spending money from your bank

account or with your credit card without your permission.

When one person usurps power and control over another through the means of finances, this is financial abuse. It can be subtle or overt, and often accompanies physical, verbal, or emotional abuse; because you have no control over finances, you can end up trapped in an abusive relationship. If you are in a situation like this, you need to get out of the relationship quickly, before the abuse escalates further.

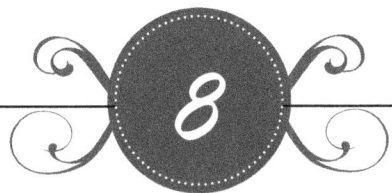

PERSONALITY AND LOVE LANGUAGES

Do opposites attract? Yes, often they do, and that's okay. You don't have to have the same personality for your relationship to work. Sometimes we think that being compatible in a relationship means having similar personalities and communication styles, but this is not always the case.

In fact, being too similar to your partner can take the spark out of the equation. A happy relationship is one in which the other person completes you, not someone who *is* you! You want someone who will make up for your weaknesses, enhance your strengths, and augment your life (and you want to be able to do the same for that special someone).

As you explore each other's personalities, communication styles, and love languages, you will notice flaws. We all have our weak spots. Learn to accept your partner for who they are, rather than trying to mold them into that dream you've crafted in your head. If there are flaws or weak spots that are deal-breakers for you, it's better to get those out in the open before you get too emotionally involved – when you can make a rational decision about whether or not to pursue the relationship.

Most of the time, however, we can learn to accept and appreciate the differences in our partners and how they help fulfill us. For instance, one of you might be high-powered and ambitious, and the other has an aura of contentment and steadiness. Rather than being irritated that the other is not as focused as you are, you can rest in the confidence that your partner is that solid rock you can lean on when you're going through challenging times.

Exploring differences in personality

We can learn a lot about our special someone's personality by simple observation as well as asking questions of each other. While exploring each other's personalities, it's helpful to understand several factors.

First, our personalities have consistency – they don't really change much over time. If you're the extroverted life-of-the-party, you'll always be outgoing to a certain extent. A more introverted person can develop social skills that help them overcome shyness and communicate better, but at their core they will prefer being by themselves or with one or two people they know well. Don't think that your partner can change their personality to please you – they won't be able to, and you'll just end up frustrated and alienated.

However, it *is* true that our personalities can be modified over time due to life experiences. For instance, someone who has gone through a traumatic experience might develop fears associated with that trauma which can make them less social. A person who lacks confidence can grow in that trait when surrounded by people who are affirming and encouraging. Alternatively, a person can develop traits of insecurity and lack of trust if surrounded by people who are sarcastic and critical or who constantly let them down. Our spirituality can have a huge impact on aspects of our personality such as how loving, joyful, peaceful and forgiving we are.

Our personalities affect our actions – how we react to situations and experiences – and they encompass our interests, decisions, and behaviors. Because no two people will have the same exact personality, you will feel differently about things and inevitably have conflict. It's more productive to learn how to manage and even embrace your differences rather than trying to change them.

When you experience conflict, don't complain about your partner's *personality* – because in doing so, you are rejecting a part of who they are. Rather, limit your criticism to specific events or issues – and work on doing it without being critical, but being a problem-solver. For instance, if your partner isn't very time-conscious and makes you constantly late to events, you can simply give an earlier time for leaving. You could say, "I'd like to leave at 5 p.m." when you really don't have to leave until 5:30. Or you could discuss it from your own perspective, "I hate running late! It makes me feel nervous and ungracious toward other people who are waiting us. Do you think we can work on that together?"

Plenty of books have been written about different personality types, and you may have gone through job-related testing and/or seminars in recognizing your temperament and how it affects your relationships, work behavior, and achievements. Of course, every expert has different ideas, but it boils down to some basic, universal concepts. Through observation and discussion, explore the following questions early in the relationship.

Introvert or extrovert?

Are you outgoing and love being the center of attention? Are you high energy and prefer being around other people? Do you tend to be upbeat, affectionate, and confident? Do you love taking control of events?

Or – are you more comfortable being on your own or with just one or two people? Do you tend to be more reserved and a bit shy, and happy to work behind the scenes? Are you introspective and thoughtful?

Open or more routine-based?

Are you a curious person? Are you always googling stuff to learn new facts? Do you have an active imagination? Do you have a deep aesthetic sense – do you long for things to be visually appealing? Are you tuned in to your own and others' feelings? Do you prefer variety and enjoy taking risks?

Or – are you thought processes more concrete than abstract? Do you prefer routine and safety? Do you like to stick with what you know and feel comfortable with?

Worrywart or secure?

Do you tend to experience a lot of anxiety, insecurity and fear about your choices, your circumstances, and your future? Do you worry about stuff a lot, and tend to be moody and pessimistic? Are you self-critical, often frustrated, envious or doubtful of others, and awkward?

Or – are you confident and secure in your choices and future, unencumbered by worry? Are you sure of yourself and fearless? Do you trust yourself and others? Are you secure enough in your own ability that you are happy, not jealous, when others succeed?

Agreeable or cynical?

Are you even-tempered, and do you feel compassion and empathy for others? Are you slow to take offense and get angry? Are you tactful, and get along well with others? Are you well-liked by others? Are you trusting of others and helpful to the point that some might say you're naïve or easily taken advantage of?

Or – are you competitive? Do you like to challenge other people and enjoy a good argument? Are you sarcastic? Do you find yourself questioning other's motives or understanding or ability? Do you tend to be a bit grumpy and insensitive to others?

Organized or impulsive?

Are you that person who's always conscientious and efficient and that everyone can depend on? Do you have self-discipline? Are you achievement-oriented and focused? Do you prefer to plan things out well in advance?

Or – are you that person who loves doing things on the spur-of-the-moment? Do you enjoy spontaneity and flexibility and living in the present, but you also tend to procrastinate? Do you tend to make quick decisions – sometimes without thinking them over well?

What about your communication skills?

Our communication skills are closely tied in with our personalities. We all have our preferred ways to communicate, and it's important in a relationship that we recognize our partner's preferred communication style and adapt to it. Below are some questions to explore, early in the relationship – mainly through observation and listening – but also ask these questions of yourself!

We can all work to improve our communication skills so that what we're trying to say is clearly understood but communicated in a non-threatening and pleasant way. If you're frustrated with your partner's poor communication skills (or they are with yours) – you can take steps to improve – such as through counseling, attending a seminar or reading through a book together on developing better ways to communicate. If your partner is unwilling to take steps to enhance communication between the two of you – you need to ask yourself what that says about the future of your relationship.

Are they a good listener?

Are they really listening, giving you their attention? Or are they often distracted with their phone or the TV? Does it seem like they are formulating their response or opinion while you're talking and/or do they interrupt you? Do they ask clarifying questions? Do they repeat back to you what they understood you to say?

Body language?

Are they relaxed and is their body turned toward you? Or do they tend to be tense or aloof, with body or head turned away? Do they make eye-contact, and use gestures such as nodding or smiling or raising their eyebrows to indicate they're listening and reacting to what you're saying?

Are they clear and concise?

Do they tend to ramble on forever, leaving you unsure of what they're actually saying? Or do they use too *few* words, so you're not able to grasp their full meaning?

Are they encouraging and empathetic?

Do they use a friendly tone and smile as you're talking with each other? Do they ask questions about your day, your visit with Mom, your problem at work, and appear interested in and supportive of what you're saying? Do they try to get a sense of how you're feeling about something and show respect for your opinions?

Proper venue and place?

Texting is fine for letting your loved one know that you're working late, or if they could run to the store for you. It's not appropriate for serious relationship discussions. Those need to be faced to face – when it's just you – when you can read non-verbal cues and hear the expression in each other's voices and touch each other. Save important talks for when you're not distracted by the big game or cooking dinner or finishing up that project before the deadline.

Do they communicate honestly?

Do you get the sense that they're not telling you the truth? Do they answer honestly, even when they feel their answer may diminish your opinion of them? Do they admit when they're at fault and apologize, rather than making excuses or (worse) blaming you for their problem?

Do they talk about little things?

Do they share with you about their day, and the funny or frustrating things that happened? Do they readily share their thoughts, opinions, and feelings?

How do you handle conflict?

Conflict is a natural occurrence in any relationship. It is not the conflict that is the problem but the way it is managed that decides the length and happiness of your relationship. Some of this depends on your individual personalities and how easily you get angry, and what you do when you have an issue with another person. So first, ask these questions of yourselves and each other:

- Do you get angry easily? What sorts of things make you angry? Do you tend to stay angry, or do you quickly forget whatever it was?
- When you do get angry, what do you tend to do? Do you say nothing but seethe inside? Do you lash out? Do you try to explain what's making you upset?
- If you've made the other person angry, do you take responsibility or simply shrug it off as they're oversensitive? Do you find it difficult to apologize?

- Are you able to forgive easily? Or do you hold grudges forever? Do you say nothing at the time but throw it in their face later, in a heated exchange? Can you forgive if the other person never apologizes? Are you sometimes *too* forgiving, and allow your partner to engage in inappropriate behaviors?

- What do you do when you don't get what you want? Do you get angry, pushy, or controlling? Or, if it's really important to you, do you explain why it's important? Do you try to negotiate – if you'll do this for me, I'll do this for you? (Doing this can make your partner feel like you are manipulating them).

- If you disagree about something, what do you do to persuade your partner? Do you try to listen carefully and find common ground and compromise a little? Do you try to take control in other ways? How open are you to looking at the other side of the argument? Is it your way or the highway? Or do you feel like you can learn from your partner's point of view?

Once you have a good idea of how each of you handle anger and apologizing and forgiveness, you can explore how you communicate and what you do when you're unhappy about something. Remember that healthy conflict management is a learned skill. This is an area that you can work on together as a couple, but both of you have to be fully committed to the process. Tips to explore about conflict management can include:

- Using "I" statements when trying to resolve a conflict is important because it removes the blame from the person and focus on the problem. For instance, if your partner has a problem making eye contact when you're talking, if you say something like, "You never look at me when I'm talking!" – you will just put them on the defensive. Instead, you could say something like, "I feel like you are not hearing me when I talk to you because you never look at me. When we're talking, I love it when we can look into each other's eyes. It makes me feel validated when you look at me. I feel like you're really paying attention!"

- Avoid the Adam and Eve blame game (it was the wife You gave me). Instead stick to expressing your feelings using "I" statements: "I feel disrespected when you don't listen to me. I would appreciate you allowing me to finish my statement." "I feel (devalued) when you (lie to me). I would appreciate if you would be (open and honest) with me moving forward."

- When your partner is speaking listen to what your partner is saying and allow them to FINISH their statement. When you interrupt your partner, you are actually saying to them that their voice doesn't matter.

- Instead of interrupting them, take notes and write down your thoughts while your partner is speaking; this will help you track the conversation better.

- Validate your partners emotions and feelings when it's your turn to speak. The purpose of validation is to acknowledge that you were listening and to communicate that their feelings are valid. An example of validation can look like this: You can *reflect the feeling* by saying, "I can see you're really upset with me because I disrespected you by interrupting you while you were speaking." This statement allows you to take responsibility and ownership to your contribution in the conflict.

- When managing conflict, it is healthy to always seek a solution. An example of this could be: "How can we heal from this?" Then together discuss healthy solutions towards moving forward.

What are your love languages?

Sometimes you can set yourself up for disappointment if you believe there are certain ways your partner should behave to make you feel valued, loved, and admired. Your partner may indeed value, love and admire you, but may not express it in the way you're expecting. This is because the two of you have different love languages. We all have ways we prefer to express love toward others or have them express it to us – ways that help us to connect emotionally.

In his book, *The Five Love Languages*, Gary Chapman explains how to give and receive love in more meaningful ways by understanding the primary love languages of one's partner. Explore these with your love interest after you've been dating for a little while and are beginning to connect on a deeper emotional level. You want to identify (for both of you) which one or two methods are most important for expressing love. Which is the most effective way for someone to express love to you, and what do you do to let that person know you love them?

- **Words of appreciation** – such as saying, "That dress looks great on you!" or "I love you!" or "I love it when you fix stuff around the house" or "This meal is really good – you're such a great cook!" If this is an important love language to you, then spoken words of affection and appreciation make you feel loved. If your partner does not verbally affirm you, or (worse yet) is critical of your efforts, you will feel unloved and unappreciated.
- **Acts of service** – such as doing something helpful for your partner – picking up a meal on the way over, washing their car, helping them with a project. This love language uses actions – usually *practical* things – to let the other know they are loved.

Often, people who prefer this love language find it hard to *speak* words of love, or to trust words of love spoken to them, but feel action speaks louder than words.

- **Giving and receiving gifts** – the gifts don't have to be expensive or elaborate, but even small gifts or flowers are the way a person with this love language prefers to express or receive love. It might be something as small as a candy bar or it might be something big – but gifts are important!

- **Quality time** – the person who values this love language wants time with just *you* – you with the phone put away and the TV off (or watching a show you both enjoy a lot) and giving them your full attention. A person with this love language may feel unloved if you get busy with work or projects and don't spend a lot of one-on-one time with them, even if you give nice gifts and words of love.

- **Physical touch** – this person craves hugs, kisses, and caresses and holding hands. This is what makes them feel loved and how they express love.

When you are exploring love languages with your partner, you might find that you have very different love languages. And that's okay! You just need to know what his or her love languages are, and act on that.

The important thing is that you are learning how to

make your significant other feel loved and appreciated. It might be completely different from how you've been doing things. For instance, maybe you've been giving lots of gifts and flowers, and all she really wants is for you to sit on the couch with her and look her in the eyes and give her your full attention! Going forward, you now know how to meaningfully express love to each other!

OUR HEALTH

oes it make you feel a bit squeamish to talk about health issues with your significant other?

If you're young and healthy, it might not even occur to you. But it's important to get out on the table any health issues that would affect a long-term relationship, even when this sort of conversation isn't as much fun to talk about.

Some examples of health issues to discuss would be any major physical health problems or mental health problems either of you might have, any addictions that might affect your health, any family health or genetic issues that might affect your loved one or your future children, and, most importantly, what each of you are doing to achieve and maintain a healthy lifestyle, and whether you are in agreement that this is an important goal to work on together as a couple.

When does one initiate these sorts of conversations? Some conversations might pop up very early on – especially your lifestyle and steps you take to promote good health. For instance, if you swim at the Y three times a week, or are addicted to Zumba, this will probably come out early on, since it's a regular part of your life. Your eating habits will also be apparent fairly soon, especially if you're avoiding sugar, or eat low-carb, or are vegetarian – or, on the opposite end of the spectrum – if you're a junk-food junkie!

Other health-related topics health might not be as obvious, and you may feel a level of discomfort discussing them, but you really do need to engage in these conversations if you see the relationship going anywhere. Maybe you're afraid of revealing a health issue because you're not sure if your partner will accept it. It's always best to be transparent about these things.

If your partner *isn't* accepting and supportive of your health problem, don't you want to know that now – before you're emotionally invested? If you wait until you're quite serious before revealing an important health issue, your significant other might feel you've been deceitful.

Eating habits and allergies?

Eating habits aren't necessarily a health issue. You might have distinct preferences for what you like to eat but still have an overall healthy eating pattern. And, for each of you, that might mean meals that are quite different. So, it's important to explore where you have common ground with regard to healthy eating, how flexible you are and open to change, and if there's anything your partner really needs to know – such as life-threatening food allergies.

Since eating together is almost always part of a dating relationship, if you have any food allergies, you need to reveal that at once, so they know not to cook anything you're allergic to, and also so they know what to do if you accidentally ingest the wrong food. If you need an EpiPen injection or antihistamine when having an allergic reaction, let your new special someone know what the symptoms look like and give instructions for what to do in case an emergency arises.

For most of us, our eating habits are a bit more mundane. For instance, we might prefer eating low-carb or engaging in intermittent fasting or eating lots of vegetables to lose weight or to lower glucose levels or to reduce inflammation. But what will you do if you're trying to eat healthy and your new love-interest does not share that goal? It's one thing to dislike broccoli, but what if they refuse to have anything green at all on their plate (except lime jello)?

And what if one of you must avoid sugar due to having diabetes or reduce salt intake due to high blood pressure? Can you work out what to do about meals? The answers to these questions will depend on your abilities to adapt and compromise, which can say a lot about how the relationship will proceed overall. It's important to remember, however, that eating habits can change, especially as we spend more time with a person.

What are your exercise habits?

If you're going to be in a long-term relationship with someone, it helps to be somewhat on the same page with them with regard to exercise. Obviously, if this relationship is proceeding to marriage, you want a long and happy and healthy life together. Exercising together – even if just a twenty-minute walk around the neighborhood each evening – can be a good way to bond and to have uninterrupted conversations, while building stronger, healthier bodies. It's helpful to find some sort of physical exercise that you both enjoy doing, to help develop positive life-long habits.

Are there physical health issues?

If you have an illness such as diabetes or a seizure disorder, you should disclose that right away when you start dating, so the other person can be prepared in case of a health emergency. You should also explain what to do in case you have an unwanted episode while with them. One young man had recently begun dating a young woman, when one evening she had a tonic-clonic (grand mal) seizure. He was terrified because he didn't know what was happening or what to do – it was all so unexpected.

After you have been dating for a little while, and the relationship is proceeding in a promising way, then the two of you need to discuss other health issues that might impact your life together – including any chronic problems like high blood pressure or thyroid disorder.

You should also discuss if you are a carrier for genetic diseases that might affect your future children – such as cystic fibrosis or sickle cell anemia. Before you marry, even though you're healthy now, you should discuss illnesses that run in your family (i.e., cardiac disease, type-2 diabetes, some types of cancer) that might possibly affect you down the road.

Mental health problems?

Mental health issues are nothing to be ashamed about and are more common than you might expect. According to the National Alliance on Mental Illness (NAMI) website, about nineteen percent of U.S. adults experienced mental illness in the year 2018 – most commonly anxiety disorders, followed by depression.

Many people, through counseling and/or medication, keep their symptoms well under control, and some even go into remission. Your mental health is a crucial aspect of who you are, and you need to share this information with each other, so you can know how to recognize symptoms, supply support, and evaluate how challenging the issue might be to your relationship. As with other sensitive issues, honesty and trust are intrinsic to building a lasting relationship.

If your loved one does suffer from a mental illness, it's important that you educate yourself about it. It's not helpful to tell someone suffering from depression or anxiety to "just snap out of it" or to "try harder." You also need to be aware of situations that might trigger problems like PTSD, and what you can do to support your partner through an episode.

Another important aspect to discuss is whether the person suffering from mental illness is taking appropriate steps to keep it under control; for instance, do they remember to take their meds? Are they sticking with counseling? Are they applying helpful techniques to reduce symptoms?

Any sexually transmitted illnesses?

Awkward, yes! But don't omit this important discussion. One young man, who'd been encouraged to date a young lady through mutual friends, told her on their very first phone call, "I don't have any social diseases." She was a bit amused by both his bluntness and the quaint language he used for STDs. But it was also comforting that he came right out and told her, especially since she was coming out of a marriage with a man who had been a serial adulterer and had infected her more than once with sexually transmitted infections he'd picked up elsewhere.

You don't necessarily need to blurt this stuff out on the first date, but any diseases that are chronic, such as genital warts, genital herpes, HIV, or Hepatitis B, need to be revealed as soon as the relationship begins to get serious (definitely before any sexual activity) – even *if* you don't have any current outbreaks of warts or lesions and even *if* your viral load is very low.

Try to hold this conversation when you're both relaxed. You can introduce the topic by saying something along the lines of, "I've been enjoying spending time with you, and I like the way this relationship is going. I feel like we can trust each other. And I'd like to share with you some personal information. I have ___ (fill in the blank) ___." Then you can explain what treatment you've been receiving, how active the disease is, and ask your partner if they have any questions.

If you *don't* have any sexually transmitted diseases, you can start the conversation pretty much the same way, but simply share that you are free from any STDs. Either way, this opens the door for your new love interest to share their own issues, if they have any. Aim at being transparent, calm, and non-judgmental.

What about addictions?

Some addictive behaviors that can negatively affect health, such as smoking, are obvious almost immediately. Others might become obvious after dating a little while – such as addictions to alcohol or drugs (prescription as well as recreational). And others, such as eating disorders, might not be apparent for some time, unless the person decides to reveal the problem.

You should know that a healthy relationship with someone addicted to alcohol and/or drugs is virtually impossible, especially if the person isn't taking responsibility and receiving help. Such people tend to engage in behaviors that are risky, illegal, manipulative, deceptive and even abusive.

You may feel like you can help this person overcome their problems, but you're more likely to get sucked into a codependent relationship. If you realize that someone you are dating is addicted to drugs or alcohol, the best thing to do is let them know you are going to "take a break" from the relationship until they get the help they need and are able to maintain freedom from addictions for a while. It's a good idea to review the "red flags for potential substance abuse" in chapter 14 if you are beginning to suspect there is a problem.

Some addictions, such as cigarette smoking, not only affect the health of the person smoking, but can also affect their partner (and any children) through passive smoking.

If one of you is a smoker, you need to have a serious discussion early on about whether or not this is a deal-breaker, whether the person is willing to quit the habit, and if not, whether they are willing to set parameters as to when and where they will smoke.

Other addictive behaviors, such as eating disorders, may not affect the relationship so profoundly; however, you should be open about any issues you have so your partner can help you avoid triggers and provide appropriate support. If you suspect your loved one might have an eating disorder, you could very gently let them know your concerns (but *not* at a mealtime) and let them know that you are there to support them and help them get the help they need.

On the topic of addictions, there are other behaviors that are not specifically health related, but that can have a serious impact on a relationship – such as an addiction to gambling or shopping. These addictions can have a devastating effect on finances as well as on the person's integrity.

If you have an addiction such as this, you really should get appropriate help from therapy and a support group before getting involved in a relationship. If you're already in a relationship, be honest with your partner about your addiction, about how it has affected finances and other areas of your life, and what you are doing to conquer the problem. Give your partner the option of "taking a break" while you go through a period of treatment.

If you're the one suspecting your partner has an addiction, bring the topic up in a manner that is calm and non-confrontational, but at the same time, be firm on where you stand, and what they need to do if the relationship is to continue.

RELATIONSHIPS
AND SEXUALITY

Earlier relationships or marriage?

*I*t's not necessary to divulge every date or short-term relationship you've ever had in your past.

However, if one (or both) of you were previously married or were in a committed long-term relationship – one that was serious enough to involve co-mingling finances or cohabitation – you should share with each other the basics of these sorts of relationships (not every little detail!) because they have had a part in shaping you into the person you are today.

You definitely don't want to compare your new boyfriend/girlfriend with someone from your past. And it's not especially productive to be super-critical of your past relationships.

Helpful information you do want to share would include whether you're still involved with that person in any way. Have you maintained a good friendship? Are you involved in business together? Do you have a child together or legal entanglements or shared debt or shared possessions or shared pets? What brought the relationship to an end? Some sort of a deal breaker? Communication problems? Infidelity? And what is the impact of your past relationship(s) on who you are today and on your current relationship.

When do you share or ask about this information? You would definitely want to know about any past marriage right away, and any children from a past relationship. If you are still close friends with a former partner or are entangled with them (i.e., shared possessions), you should divulge that early on.

Other information could be shared a bit later, as your own relationship develops. What you do *not* want to do is prattle on and on endlessly about your ex – that might lead your new special someone to think that you haven't quite gotten over the relationship. Share information that is intrinsic to your current relationship and leave the rest in the past.

Have you cheated or been cheated on?

Why would you want to share this information? If you were the one who was betrayed, you may harbor lingering trust issues or deep-seated anger that you need to work through in order to embrace a new relationship in a healthy way. Betrayals from the past can certainly affect future relationships, so it's helpful for the other person to know and understand that you may have some insecurities or bitterness that you are (hopefully) taking steps to deal with.

On the other hand, perhaps you (or your new significant other) were the one who was the cheater. It's best to share (or know about) this early on. For one thing, you may have mutual friends who might spill the beans about past infidelities.

Secondly, transparency about frailties is generally best. Did you only stray one time, or was it a habitual thing? Share *why* you cheated – not that you're trying to excuse yourself – but explain the trigger that led to cheating, and what you are doing now to overcome that character flaw. If you were a serial cheater – that's something your new significant other deserves to know.

Any sexual trauma?

If you have been happily dating for a while, to the point where you're becoming emotionally connected and contemplating a committed relationship, you should share with each other any sexual trauma inflicted from your past. The effects of sexual trauma tend to follow a person throughout their life, and may lead to debilitating issues, including fear of sexual intimacy, anxiety, post-traumatic stress disorder, depression, eating disorders, and much more.

It may be emotionally draining to share your story, and it may cause you to relive painful memories, but you each need to know this information, so the other can understand why you have certain behaviors and how to support you. You don't necessarily need to share every detail of your sad story – just sharing the highlights and the residual effect of the trauma on your life is probably enough for now. As your relationships progresses and trust deepens, you can share more if you feel led to.

If you have been the victim of sexual trauma and share your story, take note of how your partner reacts. Are they supportive, and if so, how? Do they want to run out and shoot the guy, or are they supportive of *you* – asking what they can do to help you work through the pain, and if you have any triggers they should be aware of (this is the kind of partner you want). You might get a negative reaction from your significant other – they may seem to blame you in some way or insinuate that you are damaged goods (this is the kind of partner you absolutely *don't* want).

Sexually related issues

In addition to potential sexual trauma from the past, we all probably come to the table with some sort of sexual issue, such as soul ties, addiction to porn, poor self-worth, or body shaming.

Do you have any soul ties?

As explained in chapter one, when a couple has sexual relations, even if they aren't especially committed to one another, the release of specific hormones develops an emotional bond. When two people (married or unmarried) have sexual relations, they become "one body" (I Corinthians 6:15).

You might find yourself mysteriously drawn to a person from your past that you may not have even liked very much. The relationship may have been over long ago, yet you often think about that person obsessively. You may find yourself feeling resentment toward a past sexual partner because in your mind the act of intimacy meant commitment on your part, but the other person was just taking advantage of your vulnerability.

Porn addictions

Like recreational drugs, pornography is highly addictive and can leave an imprint on your life and any relationships. Viewing porn on the internet or through reading erotic novels or other avenues can skew one's real-life sexual experiences with feelings of inadequacy or dissatisfaction, body-shaming, and more.

A man might find himself objectifying women in the way that porn depicts them. Porn addictions distort a true image of what real love looks like and what a healthy relationship of mutual respect between a man and women looks like. If you've struggled with this addition, share with your partner, along with the counseling or other steps you have taken to overcome it.

Body shaming?

Body shaming extends beyond the bedroom – we've probably all had incidents where we've been mocked or criticized or even bullied because of some aspect of our bodies – whether too tall, too short, too fat, too thin, big hips or bottom, bust too large or too small, abs not flat or muscular enough – the list can go on and on! Body shaming is so engrained in society that it can sound like truth! And often, we're the ones who are the most critical about our own bodies! For instance, those painful experiences of trying on new swimsuits!

Body shaming can affect our relationships because our body image may make us feel unworthy – and thus we might settle for whoever will accept us. It may affect our sexuality by causing us to be embarrassed to let someone else see our bodies. If you have significant issues with this, share with your new partner – not necessarily right away, but once you've begun to develop a sense of trust.

Pay attention to how supportive they are. Also, be wary of a new partner whose comments leave you with even more body-shaming or insecurities about your appearance!

Sexual identity

If you are having any struggles with whether you are heterosexual, gay, lesbian, or bi-sexual, that needs to get out in the open early on. It's not fair to the other person if one of you pretends to be heterosexual when you aren't completely sure.

Sometimes individuals from very conservative or religious or political families hide their sexual identity because they don't want to offend or disappoint their families or their faith community. Several stories have hit the media recently of high-profile individuals who were in long (and apparently happy) marriages who suddenly disclosed to their spouse (and to the world) that they were actually gay or lesbian. You can imagine how betrayed the spouse must feel and how confused the children must be.

Some adults struggle with their sexual identity due to abuse that happened in their childhood or adolescence. For instance, a woman who was physically and emotionally abused by her father may be fearful of a relationship with a man – what if the same thing happens? Or a young man who was sexually molested as a young teen may wonder if he is gay because he had an erection when a man touched him sexually. A pre-teen may have been harassed by the school bullies and called "gay" and begun to internalize their taunts. Adults who suffered abuse in their formative years should take advantage of counseling to help them work through the harm that the abuse has had on their psyche and the sexual disorientation that may have resulted.

If you have some confusion regarding your sexual identity, you should be aware that a landmark study by Harvard and MIT scientists, published in the August 2019 edition of *Science* journal,[1] refutes the idea that genetics are a primary predictor of sexual identity (i.e. you're most likely not "born" gay) and that sexuality is "shaped and regulated by cultural, political, social, legal and religious structures."

In other words, our sexual identity is more a result of what happened to us and messages we received from a variety of sources during our formative years. Your past may have confused you, but it does not define you. And not everything that was spoken over you as a child or adolescent or young adult was truth.

Gender identity

Just as with sexual identity, if you have any questions about your gender identity, or your partner's gender identity, you need to let the other person know. If you aren't sure about your gender identity, get that sorted out before pursuing a relationship. It's not fair to get involved in

---

[1] *https://science.sciencemag.org/content/365/6456/eaat7693*

a long-term relationship and then just dump that on a person after they're committed (or even married) to you.

And if you are transgender or you've had a gender change through hormones and/or surgery – that needs to be revealed right away as well – *before* you go out on a date together. This gives the other person the opportunity to either pursue the relationship or to opt out before either person gets emotionally invested. If you wait until you've been dating awhile to reveal this information (just as with a lot of other information that we've discussed), your partner is likely to feel betrayed and deceived.

Sexual proclivities

If either of you have sexual proclivities that are unusual, illegal, or considered immoral, such as pedophilia, serial infidelity, bondage, or "open relationships," you need to get that on the table right away. If you are a parent, and you suspect your new partner is attracted to your child in a sexual way, be on high alert. Get a background check done, and just flat-out ask your partner about their proclivities. Be aware that they may deny it, and the background check might not show anything, but they still may be a pedophile that has managed to stay under the radar. If you feel uncomfortable in any way, back out at once!

And if your new partner appears to have no qualms with infidelity and/or is hinting at a desire for an open relationship or doing anything else that makes you uncomfortable, let him or her know that this is a deal-breaker for you. If you discover that your new partner has proclivities that are illegal, run the other way as fast as you can. You don't want to get arrested along with that person because of some sort of sex crime and be labeled a sexual offender yourself.

Your past doesn't dictate your future.

When we are struggling with issues that affect our sexuality – such as past trauma, temptations to cheat, body shaming, porn addictions, unhealthy soul ties, or confusion on sexual or gender identity – we need to go back to the beginning. When did these issues begin? What trauma occurred or what lies were spoken over us? Is your past holding power over your thoughts and behaviors to-day? It *is* possible to change the narrative and drop the negative self-talk and that inner bully, and it *is* possible to retrain our brains and correct those distorted thoughts.

Sex before marriage

In every sort of relationship, clear communication is vital. When you begin dating, you need to each share your thoughts on sexual purity before marriage. Do you believe you should wait until you're married before having sex? If so, are you both agreed on this? Will one person try to pressure the other to go against their values?

Are each of you clear that "yes" means yes, and "no"

means no? What words or actions indicate "yes" and what words or actions indicate that things are going further than what you're comfortable with? As awkward as it is, you really want to begin discussing this very early on, so that you're not pressuring the other to go further than they want to.

You need to work on creating a culture of consent in your relationship – meaning that each respects the values that the other holds and will not try to manipulate them to do anything they're not comfortable doing.

Communicating about sex

When you are ready to commit to a life together, you need to talk about how you will discuss your sexual life together. One of the essential keys to a happy marriage is open and clear communication. As with anything else, you need to be candid and transparent about what you like and don't like, and if there are any issues that need to be addressed.

ARE CHILDREN ON THE MENU?

*W*hile it isn't exactly first-date conversation, our ideas about having and rearing children are important to share early on. You don't want to be dating for months, and thinking you've found the *one*, only to discover your partner wants a house full of kids, and you're feeling that your career and other interests would preclude having children.

Many of the following questions may or may not be deal-breakers but remember that once a couple get married and start having a family – their feelings about children might change. The person that thought they wanted four or five kids suddenly realizes that the two they already have are more than enough responsibility. Or the person who always said they didn't want kids suddenly does an about-face. But these following conversations are a good starting point.

How many children?

How do you really feel about having kids? If you want children, why? And, if not, why? How many children would you like to have? If the two of you are significantly divided on having kids or how many kids, you need to explore whether there's any room for negotiation. Do not think that after you're married, your partner will change their mind (they might, but it's not a given).

One woman had always envisioned having a large family, but when she got married, her husband only wanted two children – preferably a boy followed by a girl. And that's actually what they got. But because the woman handled birth control in that marriage, she "accidentally" conceived another child, and then another, and then another. Five in all! This created feelings of resentment in the husband regarding all the noise and expense of a large family. He lavished attention on the two oldest (the ones he wanted), and virtually ignored the younger three, except to "shush" them for being too noisy.

Timetable?

When you're planning to get married, you should discuss how long after marriage you want to wait before having children? What goals do you want to achieve first – such as completing your education or buying a house? If you want multiple children, how far apart do you think they should be spaced? What are your views on birth control?

What if you can't conceive?

How far are you willing to go if you aren't able to conceive children naturally or if you end up having recurrent miscarriages? Would you ever consider adoption or fertility treatments or hormone therapy? What are your thoughts on in vitro fertilization?

Parenting style?

Many couples don't give any thought to what their parenting styles will be until they start having children. And then, significant differences in handling disciplinary issues or in nurturing styles can lead to dissension. You don't have to both do parenting exactly the same – sometimes it's helpful to have a complementary balance – but you should agree before having children on some of the important basics. As you review the following parenting styles, the two of you can discuss which elements of parenting you think are most important.

Parenting styles are sometimes placed into four main sub-categories. Which best describes the type of parent you think you would be? As you're asking yourselves that question, also explore the type of parents your own mother and father were – because this often impacts your own parenting style. You often either model a similar parenting style as one of your own parents, or you tend to go in the opposite direction (i.e., the child of an authoritarian parent may be a permissive parent).

1. Authoritarian

These are the "strict" parents (almost military-like) – they have rigid rules for their children, and they are quick to punish if the child doesn't fall in line. They usually don't explain the reason for rules, and if questioned, will answer something like, "Because I said so." This type of parent communicates *to* the child but is not so ready to receive communication *from* the child. Authoritarian parents have high standards for their children and aren't usually very nurturing or flexible.

2. Permissive (Indulgent)

These are the "push-over" parents. They prefer to be loving and nurturing "friends" with their children, encouraging open communication, rather than telling them what to do. They don't have many rules or expectations for their children, or sometimes they *will* have rules, but tend to not enforce them because they don't want to make their kids angry or sad or break the bond between them. They don't give their children much guidance with problems or decisions – they feel it's better if kids are left to independently figure things out on their own. They tend to be permissive in allowing the kids to eat whatever they want, and don't force them to do their homework, keep their rooms tidy, or help with household chores.

3. Uninvolved

These parents are not especially involved with their children, to the point of neglect, for a variety of reasons. Some parents are more focused on their careers or personal interests and don't have much time for their children. Others may struggle with mental health or substance abuse. And others are simply disinterested in children or uncertain of what to do, so they tend to be aloof with their children.

Like the permissive parent, they don't have many rules or expectations for their children, and they pretty much let the kids do want they want and fend for themselves as best they can – often due to disinterest or lack of information in parenting skills. They typically have no idea how their child is doing in school, and don't keep up with where their child is or who they're hanging out with. Unlike the permissive parent, they have little communication with their children, and little affection or nurturing.

4. Authoritative

These parents have high expectations for their children, along with relatively strict rules – both of which are clearly explained and reasonable. The children may have some input into guidelines and what the consequences will be if they aren't followed. Authoritative parents do discipline their children, but they also praise and reward the kids when they're doing something right. Communication between parent and child is two-way, frequent, clear, positive, and affectionate, but the parent is ultimately the one in charge. Authoritative parents are warm and nurturing, and their children tend to be self-directing and have well-regulated behaviors.

Teaching children

As you and your significant other are drawing closer together and beginning to anticipate a life together, the two of you should think about and discuss how you will teach your children. For instance, how will you handle disciplinary issues? What methods will you use to correct your children? What are your views on spanking?

How will you teach values to your children, and what values would you want them to know? How and what will you teach them about God and about faith? How will you teach them life skills – such as handling finances or how to do things around the house and yard, like cooking, gardening, mowing, cleaning, sewing, and making or repairing things?

Do you already have children?

If one of you has kids, how is that working out with the dating relationship? Does the other person seem to resent the time and energy that the children take away from you? Or are they taking an interest in the children – such as asking how the soccer game went or the science project?

Once you have introduced them to the children, are they interested in "dates" that involve the kids coming along? Are they developing healthy relationships with the kids? Are they doing stuff that implies they're willing to take up the parenting role in the future – like helping them with their homework or changing diapers or bandaging a scraped knee?

When the two of you are together, how are you handling discipline? Are you okay with the other person reprimanding your child if they're out of line? And, on that topic, how evenly matched are the two of you in parenting styles – do you have similar ideas about behavior and discipline?

One young woman and her husband both had a permissive parenting style, and when they divorced, they both became even more permissive – neither wanted to be the "bad guy." Their young daughter was developing some adverse behaviors – in part because of the trauma of her parents' divorce, but also because no one ever corrected her when she was acting out.

Eventually, the mother began to date someone new,

and this man (even though he had no children of his own) was more authoritative. When he was around the little girl, he quietly but firmly told her that she could not stand on the back of the couch, that she needed to eat her carrots, and that she needed to be polite with everyone, and especially elderly adults.

At first, the child's mother was not quite sure what to think. But she eventually realized that her boyfriend was taking an interest in her child in a positive way. He was modeling an authoritative parenting style that afforded the little girl the guidance and security that she needed in a rocky period in her life. When they got married, the new husband supplied the structure and expectations that the girl was lacking, and she developed into a responsible, grounded, and loving young woman.

What if both of you have children? Do you both have full or partial custody? How close in age are the children from the two families? Have the children spent much time together? Do they get along well? How about behaviors? Do each of you feel able to deal with whatever your partner's children are bringing to the table?

Blended family

If you're seriously considering marriage, and you both have children, discuss how that will impact your living situation, your careers, your finances, and more – so much more. There are lots of confusing aspects that need to be ironed out. How involved are the other parents in the children's lives? Will you be sharing parenting, and have you met the "ex" and feel like you can work together with that person in arranging weekend and holiday schedules, paying or receiving child support, and working out differences of opinion in parenting? Who all will go to sporting events or meetings with the schoolteacher? Will it be awkward when you're all together? How much input will you have into your stepchildren's lives?

How will the children handle becoming a blended family and merging their home with other kids? Will a child who has been used to having his own room be willing to bunk with his stepbrother? If your kids are babies or toddlers, and your fiancé's kids are teens – how will that family dynamic work?

How will you handle conflicting family values or conflicts in who does what around the house – for instance, your own children are expected to make their beds, clean up their messes and load the dishwasher, but your partner's kids are used to the adults doing it all? What are your "house rules?" Is everyone willing to accept and follow them?

And how do your partner's kids feel about having you (and any kids you might have) in their life? Do they accept you? Do they respect you? Do they like you? How do your own kids feel about having your fiancé in their life? How can you strengthen the new blended family – so that everyone feels comfortable around each other and *likes* each other? What activities will draw you closer? Sit-down dinners together? Playing board games together?

And what about if the other parent of you or your partner's children isn't in the picture – through death, or abandonment, or some other sad story? How does each of you (and the children) feel about adoption of the other person's child if you get married?

When blending families – it's important to remember that you and also your children have gone through a painful process of divorce or separation – they are grieving the loss of their other parent in their lives on a daily basis. Part of the challenge of blended families is providing ways to help the children heal from the emotional wounds – so they can embrace their new life.

What can you do to help your own child – or the child of your partner feel safe and secure? How can you let them know they are valued – such as when you're making decisions that affect the whole family? What can you do to let them know you are listening to them – that they have a voice? How can you praise and encourage them? And what limits and boundaries will you expect the children to follow?

ROLES, DIVISIONS, AND DECISIONS

*I*n most marriages, fifty or one hundred years ago, there were clear distinctions between gender roles. When a couple got married, it was expected that the husband would be the primary breadwinner, while the wife ran the home and reared the children. Today, of course, gender roles have become much more fluid.

And yet, in spite of all the talk about gender equality, we still harbor ideas that *certain* things (and what those certain things *are* can change from one person to another) are meant to be done by the man and others by the woman. This can be problematic when a couple get married without a clear idea of who will assume what responsibilities in the home – in this day and age, there's no particular blueprint for which person does what – it's something you're going to have to hammer out for yourself. And some couples find themselves adjusting roles as they progress through their marriage.

It's a good idea to discuss these things long before you get married – to make sure you're more or less on the same page. Disagreements in this area are common in many marriages – you may change your minds on some things, but by discussing this before marriage – and periodically as you move through the stages of your marriage – you're heading off arguments and resentment, and you're partnering and problem-solving together.

As you begin to discuss these issues (and the time for this will be as you are getting serious and contemplating marriage, although you can bring up your opinions on gender roles much earlier), you might find that one or both of you harbor quite traditional ideas about gender roles in certain areas. Or, as you're discussing the division of labor it might seem reasonable for the person who has more skill or interest or experience in a particular area to take on that responsibility.

Sometimes work schedules will play a part – for instance, the person who gets home first might be the one who preps dinner. The important thing is that you're both happy with the arrangement, that you both feel honored and validated, and that one of you isn't shirking their duty and leaving the lion's share of labor to the other partner.

Careers, finances, and major decisions?

Will both of you work? Will one of you be the major breadwinner, and if so, who? And why? How will that change once the babies start coming? And what about when the children are all in school? Should Mom (or Dad) just work part-time or stay at home with the kids when they're little? Or do both of you intend to pursue your careers fulltime even when the children are small? And, in that case, what will you do about childcare?

How will you handle finances? Will one of you take charge of the finances and handle all the bill paying and balancing the checkbook and such? Or will you work on this together – sharing the tasks in some cooperative way? Or will you have separate finances? Be forewarned that when you get to this part of the discussion, that emotions can flare. Finances tend to be a sensitive area in general, and finances tend to be connected to control (in a number of ways), so making these decisions can be difficult.

When it comes to major decisions – such as where you will live, or buying a house, or buying a car, or making a career change – how will the two of you make such decisions? Will this be something that the two of you will discuss and come to mutual agreement on? And what happens if you can't come to a mutual agreement? Who casts the deciding vote? Or do you table the discussion?

And what about your vacations and social life? Who will decide where you go for vacation and who will make the arrangements such as booking travel and accommodations? Who will make plans for outings together or to entertain people at your home?

Who should do what?

How will you divide up the chores around the house? Who's going to repair stuff when it breaks? Who's going to mow the lawn or weed the garden? Who will take care of the automobiles? Who's going to put the furniture together once you get it to the house? And once it's put together, who decides what will go on those shelves? Who decides what color to paint the walls, and who will do the painting? Who does the cleaning, the laundry, and who buys the groceries and cooks the meals? Who cleans up after the meals? Who takes out the garbage?

There's no right way or wrong way to split up the household labor. Some couples really enjoy working together – such as cooking and doing the dishes as a team and using that as a bonding time when they can chat about their day. In other families, one person might be cooking while the other is giving the baby a bath or helping the kids with their homework.

Some couples make up a list of all the daily, weekly, monthly/as needed chores, and then each person can choose which chores they want to do. There are many ways to deal with the sharing of chores, but the important thing is that you communicate about it and come up with a plan, rather than having physical exhaustion or feelings of resentment if one person is handling most of the work around the house.

You will also need to occasionally review your plan and adapt as necessary when life changes come along – such as changes in employment, birth of children, children growing old enough to help out around the house, becoming empty nesters and so on.

And what about the children? Will you divide childcare duties (feeding, bathing, changing diapers) equally, or will one of you assume more of the responsibility? Who will take time off work when one of the kids are sick? Who's going to be buying clothes for the children or school supplies or birthday presents?

Who's going to be out in the yard teaching the kids how to swing a bat or kick a ball? Who's going to be driving those kids to their soccer games (and cheering them on), to the dentist, or to piano lessons? And what about when the children get a little older? Will you assign the children some of the household chores? Will that be tied to an allowance?

Our ideas of gender roles and division of labor may be sensitive topics, and you may find that you have differences of opinion that have probably been shaped by your own background. Be sure that you take the time to sit down together and discuss this aspect of your relationship. You will find that discussing your expectations and personal preferences will reduce stress and conflict.

FAMILIES SHAPE US

"But it's just the two of us!" you might say. "What do our families have to do with it?"

A lot! You don't exist in social isolation. Your relationship with your parents (as well as siblings and extended family) as you were growing up – and even your relationship with them now – will have a powerful impact on the quality of your marriage.

If your relationship with your family members is strained, this can undermine your relationship as a couple – both in terms of the stress of negative relationships as well as perhaps acquiring unhealthy communication habits.

If your relationship with your family members is warm and supportive, this will supply not only a good model of family dynamics, but also a sense of well-being that spills over into your own marital relationship. It's nice to have the assurance that your family is there for you to help with childcare and other needs, thus relieving many of the marital stressors.

If you suffered a lot of childhood stress – for instance, financial hardships, one or both parents with addiction issues or mental health problems, parental death or divorce, abuse, or neglect – these sorts of issues can have long-lasting effects on your sense of security, trust, self-worth, and other elements that are important for emotional health.

It doesn't mean that you can't have a happy marriage, but it does mean that you need to work harder to stay emotionally healthy, and your partner needs to understand and lend support. So, with these thoughts in mind, the two of you should share with each other your experiences with your families.

What was good? What were some of the positive dynamics that you observed between your parents, and between your parents and you (and your siblings)? What were the positive dynamics between you and your siblings? What are some of your happy memories that involved one or both of your parents? What about happy memories you have involving your siblings? Or extended family – your grandparents, cousins, aunts, uncles?

Did your parents have a good marriage? If so, what do you think made it a good marriage? How well did they communicate with each other? What things did they do to nurture their own relationship? Were they in harmony regarding their values, their opinions about child rearing, their faith, and their lifestyle?

What was dysfunctional? Was there any trauma or tragedy that affected your family? Was either of your parents an alcoholic or addicted to recreational or prescription drugs? Was there any sort of abuse (physical, sexual, verbal, or emotional) between your parents or inflicted on you and/or your siblings? Was there a lot of discord or fighting between your parents? Did they get divorced? Or were they ever married to begin with? Did something happen (such as one of your parents losing their job) that caused the family to go through serious financial stress?

Was one (or both) of your birth parents not in your life very much (if at all) – such as through divorce, death, abandonment, imprisonment, or adoption? Was there a stepparent or a partner of one of your parents that was involved in your life, and how was that dynamic? Were there any negative issues (such as abuse) with any of your extended family (grandparents, cousins, aunts, or uncles) or non-birth family (stepparent or stepsiblings)?

How did (do) your parents express love – to each other as well as to you? Go back to Chapter 8 and review the love languages. Which love language did each of your parents primarily employ when they wanted to express love to each other or to you?

Where your parents super-strict or lax with rules and discipline? Were they attentive and involved in your life, or more aloof and distant? Did you feel that they loved you and were warm and supportive? When you read through the four parenting types in chapter 11, which best described each of your parents (authoritarian, permissive/indulgent, uninvolved, or authoritative)?

What were some of the customs, practices and traditions that were (are) important to your family? How do they celebrate the major holidays? How will the two of you divide your time between families during the holidays? How were birthdays, anniversaries, graduations, and other special events celebrated? Do they have strong religious beliefs? How did that affect holidays and other traditions?

Were you and any siblings close in age, and were you emotionally close? Did you spend a lot of time playing or engaging in activities with your brothers and sisters? Did you tend to fight a lot, or did you get along well? Did you have stepsiblings or half-siblings that lived with you or were a regular part of your life? How was your relationship with them? Were you close to your cousins?

How involved are you now with your parents and siblings? Do you get along well with your parents and siblings currently, or is there discord? Do you share the same values with your parents (and siblings)?

How involved do you anticipate each of your families will be in your relationship? With any children you might have. Would they be calling and coming over all the time, or would they wait for an invitation? What would be their expectations with regard to how much time you should spend with them – seeing them every few days or at least once a week? Maybe once or twice a month…or a year? How involved do you think they will be with their grand-children when you start a family?

It's good to discuss these things with your significant other, but it's also a good idea to try to spend a good bit of time with his or her family (parents, siblings, and even extended family) to get a fuller idea of the family dynamic, because this *will* affect your own marriage.

Also, through getting to know your partner's family well, you get to know your partner better – you can see a little better *why* they might do this or that or have certain opinions or maybe even insecurities. And you also want to get a sense for how well you get along with your partner's family. You don't just marry the person – you marry the family!

GET FEEDBACK!

While you're exploring these questions with your special someone, you also want to spend time in reflection *about* that person. Try to be as objective as possible – and this is hard to do when you are falling in love with someone. But it's important to not let your emotions cloud rational thought – especially if there's something that is troubling about your partner.

One question that's important to ask yourself is, would your new love-interest get along with your friends and family? Would your parents like him or her, and why or why not? And what about your friends? If you think that they *would* like your new partner – then test it out! Introduce him or her to your family and/or your friends and see how it goes.

Just as you can learn a lot about your significant other

by spending time with their family, you can also learn more about them when they spend time with *your* family. How do they handle your own family's quirks and eccentricities? Do they seem to *like* your family and friends, and vice-versa?

Once you've introduced your new love-interest to your trusted friends and family, get feedback from them. Ask them which positive qualities they admire in that person. Ask them if they notice anything that bothers them about that person or about the dynamic of your relationship. Ask them if they see any potential red flags.

Red flags

When asking yourself and your family and friends about your new boyfriend/girlfriend, also remember to go through the "red-flags" list – characteristics and behaviors that might point toward serious problems in the person. Ask yourself these questions about your significant other, but also go through these questions with a family member or friend you can trust and who has some life experience and a good head on their shoulders. They might notice things that you're overlooking because you're emotionally involved

Red flags for potential abusive tendencies (physical, sexual, emotional, or verbal abuse)

- Do they try to dominate people – especially of the opposite sex? Are they demeaning to others?
- Do they often interrupt others, and give the impression that they think you are stupid and not worthy of having your own opinions?
- Do they tend to be obsessively competitive and get angry if they lose?
- Do they use passive-aggressive or manipulative behaviors (such as the "silent" treatment) to undermine you or downplay your opinions and feelings?
- Have they ever "gas-lighted" you? (Told outright lies to confuse you, or denied saying something you *know* they said, or told you that you're unstable – basically a campaign to make you think you're a bit unhinged)
- Do they pretend to be concerned about you, while at the same time implying that you don't measure up?
- Have they ever called you a derogatory name or made a snide comment about you in front of your family or friends?
- Are they quick to take offense or get easily angered? Is every problem your fault or someone else's fault, but never theirs?

- Are they rude, critical, or overly bossy toward the wait staff at a restaurant or the Uber driver?
- Do they tend to be violent with property – such as slamming the door or hitting the wall?
- Have they ever "lost it" and started screaming in your face? Have they ever pushed you, or slapped you?
- Do they make inappropriate jokes of a sexual nature, comment about people's bodies, or touch those of the opposite gender a little too often or in an inappropriate way?
- After a few dates, do they act like they are entitled to have sex with you, and that there is something wrong with you if you refuse?
- Are they overly jealous? Do they want to know where you are every minute, or who it is you're texting, and why you're talking to a certain person?
- Do they want you to only spend time with them, and are jealous of any time you're with your friends or family? Do they get angry if you don't respond to their texts instantly?
- Are they love-bombing you? Are they showering you with affection and extravagant gifts when your relationship is just beginning?
- Do they insinuate that they want you to be in an inclusive relationship with them, and/or to be sexually intimate right away?

- Do they often make racist, homophobic, or misogynist comments or posts on social media?

Substance abuse

- Do they have alcohol on their breath at weird times – like in the morning?
- Are they drinking more than 4 alcoholic drinks (3 for women) a day or more than 14 a week?
- Are you noticing unreliable behavior, and that they're not taking care of responsibilities?
- Do they appear physically uncoordinated or have balance issues, stumbling, or tremors?
- Are they losing weight, or have nosebleeds, or not taking care of their appearance?
- Do you ever notice red or glassy eyes, pupils dilated or slurred speech?
- Are they congested a lot, have a constant runny nose, or complain of flu-like symptoms?
- Are they jumpy, hyperactive, and speaking rapidly **or** have excessive sleepiness, are "spaced out" and speaking very slowly?
- Do you see abrupt changes in mood – bouncing from being irritable to cheerful, to aggressive, overexcited, to depressed, to agitated, to anxious or paranoid?
- Are they defensive if your try to talk about a possible addiction?
- Do you ever see burns on their lips or fingers?

- Do you notice memory issues – like forgetting conversations or commitments?
- Is it hard for them to accept personal responsibility, instead they rationalize or blame others?
- Is their job affected – has he or she been fired due to poor performance or mood swings?
- Does he or she never have enough money – may ask to borrow money?
- Does he or she smoke a lot, or routinely use tranquilizers, headache medication, or sleeping pills?
- Are they impulsive or violent?

Red flags for personality disorders, mental illness, psychopaths

- Do you see extremely impulsive and/or self-destructive behaviors in at least 2 areas: eating disorders, drinking too much, recreational drug use, reckless driving, or risky sexual behaviors?
- Do they have a poorly developed sense of self, ranging from extreme self-loathing to unrealistically high opinions of their abilities and success?
- Have they engaged in self-harming or suicidal ideations?
- Do they have extreme and unexplained irritability or anxiety that lasts hours or days?
- Do they have anger issues or rapid and dramatic changes in mood?
- Do they have a history of short romantic

relationships and/or job hopping – not being able to sustain a long-term commitment?

- Do they *not* have custody of their biological children from another relationship (especially if a female)?
- Did they adopt your family right away – calling them "Mom," "Dad," etc.?
- Do they tend to over-share – confide personal details a little too quickly or explicitly?
- Are they attracted to drama – even other people's drama – and love to play the victim?
- Do they have difficulty with logical thinking, remembering things and even speech?
- Are they hypersensitive to bright lights, certain sounds or smells and avoid places where overstimulation is likely (brightly lit stores, crowds with lots of noise)?
- Do they feel disconnected from others and from their environment, as if everything is unreal?
- Are they fearful or suspicious of others?
- Do they give an overly high priority to money, power and winning?
- Do they feel that moral or social rules do not apply to them?
- Have you seen dishonest and/or manipulative and/or bullying behaviors?
- Do they have a lack of empathy for others, and a

lack of remorse for their actions? Are they cold and calculating?

- Do they exhibit low impulse control – acting first and thinking later?
- Are they narcissistic, self-centered, and extremely sensitive to criticism?
- Have you ever seen them be cruel to animals?

Red flags suggesting the person is hiding something

- They never have you over to their place.
- You've never met anyone in their family.
- They're off the grid – no Facebook, Twitter, Snapchat, or other social media presence.
- They never talk about their childhood or even their more recent past.
- You don't really know very much about them.
- They disappear for days at a time, and/or call or text you very late at night.
- They're overly protective of their cell phone – they don't want you to see what you're doing on it.

Red flags for financial issues

- They have enormous student loan debt and/or student loans in default.
- They have over $10,000 in credit card debt that they're not doing anything about (except maybe

continuing to spend); they only pay the minimum payment each month.

- They have a past bankruptcy.
- They have a history of job hopping or often get laid off from jobs.
- They have a shopping addiction.
- They spend more than they earn.
- They have no sense of saving for retirement or more immediate goals.
- They like gambling – a lot.

Red flags for a pedophile

- They spend a lot of time with a "favorite" child.
- Not a parent, but he or she often volunteers with children or babysits children (not a problem in and of itself but could be if other red flags here are evident).
- He or she is overly physical with children – touching a lot – hugs, tickling, wrestling, having them sit on lap – even if child has indicated discomfort.
- You notice them staring at a child for a long period.
- He or she makes inappropriate comments about a child's appearance.
- They insinuate that they have "rights" over other people.
- They are highly interested in your child's life and seems highly interested in what your child likes

(once again, not an issue by itself, but could be if other red flags are evident).

- Laughs at you for being a "helicopter parent."
- Offers to give rides to your child or babysit them (when very new in relationship).
- Offers to have child stay overnight with them.
- Suggests that your child has a problem with lying (which may cast doubt if the child reports abuse).
- Doesn't respect privacy of child when the child is dressing or going to bathroom.
- Frequently watches porn, and especially child porn (which, of course, is illegal).

Red flags for a serial cheater

- Is he or she "cushioning" – dating you, but continuing to text and flirt with others, or maybe even hanging out with others – keeping them on the "back burner" just in case your relationship flames out?
- Do they have a history of "catch and release" – dating someone and then letting them go for a "better" option?
- Is he or she "micro-cheating" – little things like still texting the ex – still has a need to seek attention outside your relationship?
- Is he or she a player? Are they super-charming and make you feel like you're the only person in their life one day and then ghost you the next? Do their

words sound like they're ready to commit, but in reality, they're not emotionally connected?

- Pay attention to what his or her family and friend say about your love-interest – and their past relationships. Were they all short-lived?

A BACKGROUND
CHECK?

"What! A background check for someone I'm interested in dating. Isn't that over the top?" This may be your initial reaction; however, think of the reasons that backgrounds checks are usually done: for many jobs (especially jobs involving children or finances), before going into business with someone, when applying for guardianship of a minor child or disabled adult, when applying to be a foster parent or to adopt a child.

Now, think about what marriage involves – your finances, your children (current or future), and essentially everything else for the rest of your life. Why waste time dating someone that isn't marriage material? And if you already have children, why bring someone into their life who might not be safe?

When is it a good idea?

A background check is always recommended if you already have children – you are responsible for protecting them from sexual offenders and/or individuals with a history of violence or instability (including financial instability).

A background check is also a good idea if this is a person that no one in your circle of friends and family and co-workers knows – for instance, if he or she is someone you've met online, or at a party or just randomly somewhere. Even if you or other people in your circle do know him or her, how well do you or they know them? Is this just someone you know very casually from work or the friend of someone's friend?

If you (or a friend or family member you trust) have not known this person well for an extended period, it never hurts to do a background check. And, once you begin dating, if something problematic pops up (like one or two of the red flags from the earlier chapter), or you just have a sense that something is "off" – it's well worth the investment.

When should it be done?

If this is a case of someone you don't know well, you probably should do at least a basic (free – see below) background check before going out with them the first time. If you have minor children, you definitely should check the sexual offender list and do a basic check (followed by a more extensive one if anything pops up) before you ever introduce this person to your children.

As the relationship progresses, if any red flags emerge, do one at once. It's a good idea to do a check of their financial history if you're going to be co-mingling finances in any way. You can use several methods (many free) for checking out a person's character and background.

Basic freebie checks

- **Sexual Offender List:** You can check out whether someone is registered as a sexual offender by going to the National Sex Offender Public Website and putting in the person's name and their county of city of residence and then requesting a search for all states.

While you're on that site, you can also check out if any sexual offenders are in your neighborhood by doing a search by address radius; however, not all states have the geographical coordinates for that type of search (but you can get results from the Neighborhood Watch or Family Watchdog sites).

- **Scope out their Facebook and other social media sites**: Obviously, people usually manage their Facebook and other social media to put their best face forward. However, perusing their sites can supply quite a bit of information, depending on how much they put out there – such as their past relationships, employment (past and present), interests, morality, political leanings, faith and much more.

Of course, you have to remember that a lot of this is what they're saying about themselves, but taking a look at the types of things they post (and the comments that people leave and way they interact with people that comment on their posts) can give you a general idea of the person. If their Facebook is set to private, send a "friend" request – which they should honor if they're interested in dating you (and of course that means they'll have access to your own Facebook page).

- **Google them**. Enter their full name in quotation marks (i.e., "Jason Banks" or "Jessica Ann Brown"). If it's a fairly common name, narrow down the search by including the city of residence (and past locations). This will usually bring up any work-related profiles they have (such as Upwork or LinkedIn) and social media sites where they're using their real name (a lot of people use a nickname or just their first name for social media, but a google search might pull them up anyway, and then you can do another search using their nickname).

It should also pull up basic "White pages" or "Been Verified" or "My Life" sites that will list their age, current city and state, previous cities where they've lived, and family members (and there's a paid option for a more extensive check). The "My Life" site will list if they have an arrest record or a lawsuit/lien/bankruptcy record on the "free" check, but not the details of what it is (you can check that out through their paid option).

More extensive paid background checks

If you've already pulled up "White pages," "Been Verified," "My Life" or other similar sites, they will offer you a more extensive check (which will usually include information such as warrants, arrest records, convictions, incarcerations, court records, government license information, weapon permits, foreclosures and bankruptcies, marriages and divorces, and property ownership) for prices ranging from around $10 to $40. The Criminal Watchdog website answers a lot of questions about types of background checks and prices (and they also offer their own for various prices). You can also access sites like Intelius or Truth finder.

What will a background check not tell you?

Most background checks won't supply extensive information (if any) on past employment or education. Not all criminal information will necessarily show up – for instance, offenses committed as a minor or that were expunged, older records (in many states), or records on the federal level (rather than county or state).

Also, many states only report convictions, not arrests (a person can commit a crime, get arrested, but not convicted due to insufficient evidence). Usually, the only financial information you can see are things like bankruptcies or home ownership or other public information, so you wouldn't know if they have massive debt or other financial issues that would only show up on a credit report (which can only be obtained with the person's permission and cooperation).

Also, a person may have been flying under the radar, so to speak. For instance, they may have sexually molested a family member or an acquaintance, but the family or acquaintance did not report it, so they aren't on the sexual offender list. They may have been arrested for rape or assault or any number of things, but if the prosecutor lacked enough evidence, it may not have gone to trial, or the case may have been dismissed, in which case many states won't report it (although by googling the person, you might find news accounts of any arrests).

Conclusion

If you've made your way through this book, your head may be reeling with all the considerations involved when dating and contemplating marriage. Yes, it can be overwhelming! And yet, you now have the secret to building an enduring, passionate, healthy relationship. You've been empowered in how to proceed in an intentional way and learned how to protect yourself from potential harm and heartbreak You have learned to be real about who you really are and how to discover who your partner really is. You have the indispensable key to figuring out if your partner is *the one.*

If you're not currently dating someone, this book is your guide for what to look for, so you can find someone who is a great fit for you. And then, as you proceed through your relationship, you can explore these topics together and build a loving and enduring relationship.

And if you are currently in a relationship, it is my prayer that this book has helped you initiate and shape informed, honest and open dialogues that have helped you learn about each other. Perhaps these questions have opened your eyes to areas where you need to negotiate and compromise. Ultimately, I hope it has given you confidence that the two of you can step into a marriage that is happy and whole. May you be blessed in your journey!